REMEMBERING OUR PAST

HOUSTON RACQUET CLUB 50TH ANNIVERSARY

CELEBRATING OUR FUTURE

50 REMEMBERING OUR PAST

HOUSTON RACQUET CLUB 50TH ANNIVERSARY

CELEBRATING OUR FUTURE

HOUSTON BUILDS A RACQUET CLUB

An artist's conception of the Houston Racquet Club to be completed in the spring of 1968 depicts the contemporary design adapted to the beautiful wooded, rolling site on Memorial Drive near Voss Road.

The Houston Racquet Club has let contracts for construction of a magnificent $1,750,000 new club. The contract for the clubhouse construction was let to T. D. Howe Construction Company of Houston.

The building and grounds, set on a beautiful wooded, rolling site on Memorial Drive near Voss, were designed and landscaped by MacKie and Kamrath, Architects. Advantage was taken of the undulating terrain by placing tennis courts on different levels.

The contract for construction of the AAU size swimming pool was awarded to the Abernathy Company. Announcement of both contract awards was made by Ken Burroughs and George Mitchell, co-chairmen of the club's building committee.

A large initial membership was caused partially by a merger with Sagewood Country Club. However, the increased demand for memberships soon resulted in a waiting list. A recent Racquet Club Board of Directors meeting voted to increase membership from 800 to 1000. Applications are currently being accepted.

Originally formed to fulfill a need in Houston for a private tennis club, the Racquet Club will soon be in a position to entertain major international events in professional tennis.

Plans call for 18 tennis courts at first, with projections for a total of 31 courts at a later date. Ultimately, the club will feature air-conditioned courts for night and day play. There will also be two handball courts which can also be used for squash.

The clubhouse will comprise about 36,000 square feet and will be designed on four levels to conform to the landscape. It will be constructed of organic material to blend with the surrounding area.

Up half a flight from the entrance and lobby will be the main ballroom, cocktail lounge and dining area. The ballroom will have a long, glassed-in balcony overlooking tennis courts and a beautiful terraced ravine.

Other levels will contain private dining rooms, the mixed grill, a bar, locker rooms with showers, saunas and massage areas, a snack bar and the handball courts.

The club is made up of many members of Houston Tennis Patrons, Inc., the organization that sponsors free tennis lessons for Houston youngsters during the summer months, and organized tennis youth league play.

Completion of the new Racquet Club is scheduled for spring, 1968.

THE HOUSTON RACQUET CLUB MISSION

"The Club for a lifetime! To instill, inspire, and promote love and enjoyment of the game of tennis; to encourage athletic and social fitness activities in an exceptional family environment; and to satisfy the social, recreational, and fitness needs of its members in a congenial atmosphere."

▲
2007,
HRC Resort Pool

Houston Racquet Club
10709 Memorial Drive, Houston, TX 77024
www. houstonracquetclub.com
713-464-4811

ISBN: 978-0-9965408-0-3

Printed in the United States of America by
Bayside Printing Company, Inc.
First Edition

In the making of this book, every attempt has been made to verify names, facts and figures. We apologize for any errors.

Publishing Consultant, Book Production, Research and Writing
Roni Atnipp

Book Design
Limb Design – Houston, TX – Linda Limb and Elise DeSilva

Editing
Doug Williams

Proofreader
Polly Koch

Cover Photograph and Chapter Pages
Terry Vine Photography - Terry Vine

Back Cover Photograph
Micahl Wyckoff

TABLE OF CONTENTS

THE NET SET

50¢

Nov. '67

▶

1967, *The Net Set* magazine cover, Looking over building plans: LtoR, Kenneth Burroughs, Co-chair of the Building Committee; William Black Jr., Club Treasurer; Karl Kamrath Sr., Architect; Joel Howard Smith, former First Vice President

FOREWORD

Celebrating milestones is important not only to remember and honor achievements, but also to take time to look back at how the dreams were born and how those dreams helped to shape the future.

For two years, the Houston Racquet Club's 50th Anniversary Committee has been meeting every month to discuss plans to commemorate the Club's birthday. The 50th year festivities started in January, when we held the largest event in the Club's recent history – a kickoff party attended by over 800 members. April saw an exhibition tennis tournament that brought back HRC's four original head tennis pros. And in June, HRC put on its first-ever Kids' Carnival, which had everything from fried Twinkies and cotton candy to giant slides and games. In October, the Club had the most lavish gala weekend since its Grand Opening Gala in 1969.

The Anniversary Committee also took on two more permanent projects conceived to stand the test of time: a pathway to be built with bricks engraved with members' names, and this coffee table history book filled with the story of HRC and its fascinating past. The book is a celebration of the spirit of our founders, the dedication of our members throughout the years, and the commitment of our staff, who keep the Club going day in and day out.

We would like to take this opportunity to thank everyone who has helped in the planning process that has made our anniversary year such a success. We are truly proud to be members of such a unique and outstanding club.

50TH ANNIVERSARY COMMITTEE

Roni Atnipp
Chair

Mitch Creekmore	Cathy Lassetter	Bambi Schuette	Bob Stagg
Tom Eaton	Ron Latta	Bob Shealor	Mindy Voyles
Ron Fisher	Ryan McCleary	Adelaide Smith	Kathy Zay
	Leland Putterman	Meg Smith	

Thomas Preuml, CCM – COO/General Manager
Sonny McDaniel – Assistant General Manager
Alisha Kato – Director of Catering
Jean Northey – Executive Assistant

$1 Million Racquet Club Slated

STUDY A
HOUSTON RACQUET CLUB
MACKIE & KAMRATH AIA
ARCHITECTS

SCHEME A

ARCHITECT'S SKETCH OF NEW 31-COURT HOUSTON RACQUET CLUB

The Post Sports

CLARK NEALON, SPORTS DIRECTOR   **MICKEY HERSKOWITZ, SPORTS EDITOR**

PAGE 1, SECTION 4   WEDNESDAY, NOVEMBER 24, 1965

31 Courts, Clubhouse, Pool, Stadium Planned

By JACK GALLAGHER, Post Sports Writer

Plans were announced Tuesday for the $1 million Houston Racquet Club, a private tennis club located on a 12-acre site at Bingle Road south of the intersection of Katy Freeway.

The first of its type in Texas, the non-profit corporation will have 31 tennis courts, including two air-conditioned courts lighted for night play.

FACILITIES WILL also include a two-level air conditioned clubhouse, a 2,000-seat tennis stadium and an AAU-sized swimming pool.

James A. Walsh is chairman of the board of directors. Some 150 Houstonians have already joined the club, and applications are being processed from 50 additional members.

"I don't think we'll have any trouble getting the required minimum of 300 members," said Walsh.

"Our club will be a family-type operation for the purpose of developing and enjoying tennis, swimming and social activities. This is for the people who can't afford to join a golf club, where tennis sometimes gets second-class treatment."

THE RACQUET Club will easily be the largest tennis facility in Houston. There are 18 courts on the eight acres at Memorial Park.

"We'll be the first club with air conditioned courts," said Walsh. "In fact, the only other air conditioned court I know of is on the private residence of Al Hill in Dallas."

Three - fourths of the 31 courts at HRC will have composition surfaces. The remainder will be of Laykold.

The firm of MacKie and Kamrath, which designed the Memorial Park Tennis Center, has been retained as architects.

"HOUSTON HAS long needed a facility of this type," said geologist George Mitchell, a member of the board of directors. "Jackson, Miss., a town of 200,000 people, has a similar operation to the one we plan. There are three country clubs in Jackson, but the tennis club has 650 members."

Other members of the HRC's board of directors are R. H. Baker, William B. Black Jr., Jack S. Blanton, R. R. Cravens, Dr Thomas D. Creekmore, Karl Kamrath Sr, Robert W. Kurtz, Howard Startzman and Joseph H. Stevens.

Bylaws provide for 800 voting memberships, 50 non-resident memberships and 50 junior memberships for members 21 to 30 years of age. The 250 charter voting memberships will cost $600, the second 100 $700, the third 250 $800 and remaining 200 $1000.

Completion of Phase I, consisting of the clubhouse, swimming pool and 15 tennis courts is scheduled for the summer of 1966.

Further information on memberships can be obtained by phoning or writing James A. Walsh at the Underwood Neuhaus & Co.

INTRODUCTION

Fifty years ago, George Mitchell and a small group of men had a vision of creating a premier tennis club in the Memorial area of Houston. Their unwavering commitment to realizing that vision – and the determination of subsequent leaders and members to build upon it – has made the Houston Racquet Club one of the finest tennis and fitness facilities in the United States.

I am honored to serve as President of HRC during our 50th anniversary year celebration. The Club continues to flourish, with over 1,400 members and their families enjoying the tennis, social, and fitness opportunities that were at the core of our founders' aspirations a half-century ago. And while I recognize that we have come a long way over the years, I cannot help but think that HRC's best days are still ahead.

I want to thank the 50th Anniversary Committee, especially Roni Atnipp, for all their hard work on this commemorative book. It richly chronicles the history of our Club and provides our members with a wonderful opportunity to appreciate and reflect upon HRC's tradition and history. But more than that, it is truly a deserving celebration of our past, present, and future.

Regards,

Bradford Patt, MD
Houston Racquet Club President 2014-2015

GEORGE BUSH

February 2015

Congratulations on the Houston Racquet Club's milestone of fifty years of serving your membership and the community with tennis, fitness and friendship.

It seems like a million years ago that I helped dedicate the new Houston Racquet Club with the purpose of inspiring participation in recreational and competitive tennis, both locally and nationally, in these exceptional surroundings.

As you look back on your accomplishments and share in fellowship, it is also an opportunity to look to the future. Though my legs no longer allow me to play the sport I so loved for much of my life, I still believe tennis is a family sport to be enjoyed at just about any age. Few clubs or organizations do more to promote this concept of tennis than does the Houston Racquet Club.

And they make a very fine bowl of chili to boot!

So it is with gratitude and appreciation that Barbara and I send congratulations to the members, Board of Directors and Founders of the Houston Racquet Club.

Sincerely,

G Bush

THE NET SET

50¢

Jan. '70

1970, *The Net Set* magazine cover,
The Honorable George H.W. Bush
when he was
U.S. Representative Bush

1973

Davidson retires, and Sammy Giammalva is hired as next Head Tennis Pro

1977

Lecher leaves, and Horst Manhard is hired as next HRC General Manager

1981

HRC adds new courts for a total of 41, with 25 clay and 16 hard courts

1974

Wiedower retires, and Kurt Lecher becomes next HRC General Manager

1976

World Oilman's Tennis Tournament (WOTT) is established at HRC

Giammalva retires, and Jimmy Parker is hired as next Head Tennis Pro

1980

Major renovation of Dining Room and Grill is completed

1984

Sherman Hink starts "King of the Hill"

1965

Houston
Racquet Club is
incorporated

1967

Construction is finished on
six HRC tennis courts and
a small pro shop

1969

March 7-9, is HRC's Grand
Opening Gala dedication weekend

HRC swim team is formed with
147 swimmers, 10 meets / 8 wins

1971

HRC hosts first National Senior Women's
Clay Court Championships

1966

HRC votes to drop option on Voss Road
location

HRC votes to move to current location
on Memorial Drive in
Hunters Creek Village

HRC executes merger with
Sagewood Country Club

Dean Wiedower is hired as first Club
General Manager, and Richard Nesmith
is hired as first Tennis Pro

1968

Head Tennis Pro
Jerry Evert is
hired

Women's Association
is formally organized

1970

"Original 9" start the
Virginia Slims Tour at HRC,
originating the Women's
Professional Tennis Tour

1972

Evert retires, and
Owen Davidson is hired as
next Head Tennis Pro

TIME
1965

LINE
2015

2008

Griffin leaves, and Thomas Preuml is hired as next COO/General Manager

Hurricane Ike hits, and Club closes for two weeks

HRC is awarded USTA "Club of the Year"

2012

Men's Association is established

2006

Parker retires after 30 years at HRC, and Thomas Cook is promoted to next Head Tennis Pro

Grand Opening celebration of major renovation projects is held on May 26

2009

Major erosion occurs after heavy rain; repair work begins on Soldiers Creek

2015

Membership votes to approve HRC expansion and renovation and first assessment

Conceptual View of the Adult Dining Bar/Lounge

50th Anniversary

1993

President George H.W. Bush and Barbara are given an honorary HRC membership

HRC is declared as smoke free with only a few designated smoking areas

2004

Phase I renovation begins with ballroom, Grill, kitchen, and entrance

1989

HRC's first Fitness Center is opened – located where Kids' Club is now

1985

Sally Tinkham becomes first woman elected to Board

BOARD OF DIRECTORS 1987-1988
Earle S. Alexander, Jr., *President*
Robert B. Sale, Jr., *Vice President*
Roger A. Anderson
Clyde G. Buck
Jack D. Childers
Myrven H. Cron
David L. Deane
James L. Dougherty
Walter R. Evans
William F. Howell
Robert N. Landauer
Jim LaRoe
R. M. (Monty) McDannald
Judge Michael T. McSpadden
Sally G. Tinkham
Sterling F. Womack
Thomas D. Creekmore, D.D.S., *Ex-Officio*

1991

Grill area construction projects and improvement of balcony seating are completed

1995

Ballroom is remodeled

2005

Phase II renovation begins with resort pools, Pavilion, basketball area, parking, and Fitness Center complex

Manhard retires after 28 years, and Steve Griffin becomes next General Manager

Meg Smith is elected first HRC female president

DEDICATION TEXT
HOUSTON RACQUET CLUB

To PROVIDE INSTRUCTION AND PARTICIPATION IN RECREATIONAL AND COMPETITIVE TENNIS AND A FRIENDLY ASSOCIATION IN THESE EXCEPTIONAL SURROUNDINGS

To INSPIRE AND PROMOTE LOCAL AND NATIONAL INTEREST IN THE GAME OF TENNIS

To TENNIS - THE FAMILY SPORT OF A LIFETIME!

To THESE ENDS MAY THE BLESSING OF GOD BE UPON THE SUCCESSORS TO THE FOUNDERS:

KENNETH R. BURROUGHS   GEORGE P. MITCHELL
KARL KAMRATH SR.   JOEL HOWARD SMITH
HUGH E. McGEE JR.   JAMES A. WALSH

CHARTERED MAY 5, 1965
OPENED MARCH 7, 1969

MacKIE & KAMRATH A.I.A.   T. D. HOWE CONST. CO.
ARCHITECTS   CONTRACTORS

CHAPTER ONE

THE EARLY YEARS – A CLUB FOR THE FUTURE

HIS MISSION WAS SIMPLE: TO CREATE A
TENNIS CLUB THAT WOULD PROMOTE FITNESS.

LONG BEFORE HE WOULD BECOME A LEGEND IN THE MODERN ENERGY WORLD, GEORGE MITCHELL WAS SHAPING A WHOLE DIFFERENT KIND OF LEGACY.

It was 1964. Mitchell, who would later be credited with inventing the technology that ushered in America's 21st century oil and gas boom, had just returned from New Orleans, Boston, and Jackson, Mississippi, where he'd been looking at tennis facilities. His mission was simple:

To create a tennis club that would promote fitness.

A Galveston-born wildcatter who would later develop The Woodlands, Mitchell was no latecomer to the sport. He had been the captain of Texas A&M University's tennis team in 1940 and believed strongly that the emerging age of television sports ran the real risk of creating a nation of spectators. The regular exercise that tennis offered could counteract the "couch potato" syndrome by delivering significant health benefits – especially to those over 40.

Although his vision was somewhat novel for the times – golf, not tennis, had traditionally been the focus of "country clubs" – Mitchell pressed on. He signed a $7,500 option to buy 10 acres of land bordered by Voss Road and the Katy Freeway that would serve as a potential site for the Club.

A year later, he and a founding group made up of members of the Houston Tennis Patrons and the Houston Tennis Association formally established the Houston Racquet Club. The first Board consisted of Mitchell, Ruddy Cravens, James A. Walsh, Tom Creekmore, Karl Kamrath Sr., R.H. Baker, William B. Black Jr., Jack S. Blanton, Robert W. Kurtz, Howard Startzman, and Joe Stephens. It wasn't long before the newly christened Club had 400 members.

Meanwhile, Sagewood Country Club – which had been chartered in 1951 as a private club – had been looking for a newer, larger location. Sagewood had started relatively small, with just a clubhouse, a swimming pool, and a few tennis courts, but its membership had outgrown the facility by mid-decade.

When the 1960s arrived, the debate over Sagewood's future focused on three possibilities: sell the Sage Road location; expand the existing club to include a golf course; or make the necessary changes to preserve Sagewood as a tennis club.

The third option prevailed. Sagewood and the Houston Racquet Club merged.

March 1969, View of the Clubhouse from Memorial Drive

March 7, 1969, Founding members of HRC in attendance at the Grand Opening Gala:
Back LtoR, Joel Howard Smith, Hugh McGee Jr., James Walsh;
Front LtoR, George Mitchell, Karl Kamrath Sr., Kenneth R. Burroughs

It quickly became clear that the 10 acres Mitchell had originally optioned would not accommodate a combined membership that suddenly numbered 800. So that plan was dropped, and HRC's leadership set out to find more space.

The search didn't take long.

As it happened, Houston realtor Conrad Bering told Mitchell that the 17-acre estate of Carroll Delhomme, located off Memorial Drive, was for sale. Not only that, but Mitchell's business partner, George Butler, owned land next to the site. The two tracts totaled 26 acres and carried a price tag of $338,000.

The Houston Racquet Club had found a home.

Mitchell and the Club leaders worked out the logistics to combine the two sites and win approval from the city of Hunters Creek, and proceeds from the sale of Sagewood Country Club were used to buy the properties. With the land secured, attention turned to the buildings that would grace it. Within a few months, construction began on six hard courts at the end of a long driveway through the woods of the HRC property to allow tennis play to begin. Reservations and equipment were kept in what was affectionately known as the "shack," and drinks were sold to members out of an ice cooler.

At this point, the Club put to use the architectural talents of Karl Kamrath Sr.

Kamrath was an ideal fit for the Club. A competitive tennis player since his childhood, he became the NCAA Doubles Champion while a student at the University of Texas. He was on the HRC's first Board. And by the mid-1960s, he had become a widely known and respected architect, devoted to the style of Frank Lloyd Wright, and his artistry was on display in structures that included the Humble Oil Building, Memorial Drive Presbyterian Church in Bunker Hill Village, and the University of Texas School of Public Health building.

Who better than a tennis-playing architect to design a tennis club that would be unmatched in Houston?

Initially, Kamrath was to create a clubhouse of between 15,000 and 20,000 square feet that would accompany 10 to 12 tennis courts. But HRC's members and leadership were committed to having a premier facility that was "second to none." So a new dues structure was approved that allowed for a clubhouse twice the size of the original concept and a total of 26 courts.

With Kamrath's new design in hand, construction began in 1968 and was completed in time for a March 1969 dedication that featured then-Congressman George H.W. Bush as guest of honor. A huge tennis fan and regular player himself, the man who would become the nation's 41st President officially dedicated the Club in a grand ceremony and gala event.

But no sooner had the Club's first chapter come to an end than the second chapter began to unfold. And what had begun as George Mitchell's plan for a tennis-focused club was about to become much, much more.

Artist rendering from an
early HRC brochure

Winter 1973, HRC Clubhouse
construction

GEORGE P. MITCHELL

He was born George Phydias Mitchell on May 21, 1919, in Galveston, Texas. He was an American businessman, real estate developer, and philanthropist who is credited with pioneering the economic extraction of shale gas – today known as hydraulic fracturing. He became interested in tennis as a child and began competing in tournaments in Galveston. As a senior at Texas A&M University in 1940, he was captain of the tennis team and graduated first in his class in petroleum engineering.

After the war, he settled in Houston with his wife, Cynthia, and started an independent oil and gas company, Mitchell Energy & Development Corp., which became a Fortune 500 company. In 2007, he was inducted into the Texas Tennis Hall of Fame for his contributions to the game.

He was the father of 10 children. On July 26, 2013, Mitchell passed away at his home in Galveston at the age of 94.

His family statement on the George and Cynthia Mitchell Foundation website says:

"He will be fondly remembered for flying in the face of convention – focusing on 'what could be,' with boundless determination – many times fighting through waves of skepticism and opposition to achieve his vision.

"Whether it was graduating first in his class at Texas A&M University, developing The Woodlands, a master-planned new town, pioneering the technology that unleashed the shale gas boom, working to create a more sustainable planet, restoring the historic area of Galveston, or just fishing with his family, he had the right mix of vision, optimism, and tenacity, and a love for his fellow man.

"We are and will forever be grateful for the gift of this remarkable life. There's no doubt that he helped make this world a better place."

March 7, 1969, George Mitchell at the HRC Grand Opening Gala

September 2009,
George Mitchell at the
HRC Past Presidents Dinner

MITCHELL'S VISION

"Tennis at that time was still an amateur sport with a relatively small base of players. The Open Era, which was to profoundly impact the sport, was still a couple of years in the future, and the flood of money, media attention, and consequent new players it would bring was still unforeseen. So there was no guarantee that a tennis club modeled after a country club with no golf could survive."

- Jimmy Parker – HRC Head Tennis Pro 1976-2006

HIS DREAM

"When Tim Purcell and I met with George Mitchell about our Club in 2009, it was evident Mr. Mitchell had a great deal of passion for tennis and the Houston Racquet Club. He quickly explained, 'When we started HRC, our vision was to create an environment of family around tennis. That was many years ago! Today, clubs must adapt to the ever-evolving needs of a modern family, such as providing fitness and recreation – and HRC has done that with top-notch facilities.'"

- Steven Madden – HRC President 2009-2010

HIS GAME

"When George Mitchell was in town, he played every weekday at four p.m. One day there was a gas leak near the Club and the police closed us down. George showed up to play. I asked him how he got in, and he said, 'Oh, I know the police. They let me through.' No one else was there, so he played with the janitor."

- Horst Manhard – HRC General Manager 1977-2005

HIS COMPETITIVE EDGE

In his obituary from the *Houston Chronicle*, his family reminisced, "He remained a competitive player into his 70s and three days a week he could be found at HRC in his 4 o'clock match. He challenged his children, promising a reward for anyone who could beat him in tennis before he turned 60. No one did, and that included several who played on high school tennis teams. He extended the challenge to age 65 for lack of serious competition."

HRC GRAND OPENING GALA

HRC's Grand Opening Gala took place on Friday, Saturday, and Sunday, March 7-9, 1969

Friday night's opening ceremonies included a cocktail party and seated dinner for 460 people at the Clubhouse with dancing that lasted until one a.m. to the music of Buddy Brock and his 18-piece orchestra. The evening kicked off with the introduction of the six founding members: George Mitchell, current President; James A. Walsh, First President; Hugh McGee Jr., Second President; Karl Kamrath Sr.; Kenneth R. Burroughs; and Joel Howard Smith.

A welcome address was given by President Mitchell, after which then-U.S. Representative George H.W. Bush spoke. In his opening speech, Congressman Bush said he had "escaped momentarily from Disneyland East" and stressed that "others around the United States will emulate what we have done here." Bush continued that tennis should be a sport emphasized in Houston. As an example, he suggested the creation of more amateur tennis leagues, such as those initiated by the Houston Tennis Patrons, and holding a $25,000 pro-amateur invitational tournament.

Congressman Bush delivered the following dedication:

"By the powers given to me by the Founders, the Officers and Directors, I do hereby dedicate the Houston Racquet Club:

"To providing instruction and participation in recreational and competitive Tennis and a friendly association in these exceptional surroundings.

"To inspire and promote local and national interest in the game of Tennis.

"To TENNIS – The Family Sport for a Lifetime!

"To these ends, may the Blessings of God be upon the successors to the Founders.

"By these powers, I hereby call upon George Mitchell, as President of the Houston Racquet Club, to have this dedication cast in a plaque of suitable design, to be permanently affixed in a prominent location on the Houston Racquet Club premises for all to see and remember."

This was followed by a blessing from the Rev. Thomas Bagby, Rector of St. Martin's Episcopal Church. After the blessing, everyone joined in to sing "God Bless America" and "The Eyes of Texas."

Saturday night's festivities were attended by about 650 people and included a buffet of hors d'oeuvres and dancing until one a.m. featuring music by Ed Gerlach and his 15-piece orchestra. Before the dancing began, the players in Sunday's exhibition match were introduced: Bob Lutz and Stan Smith, the U.S. Davis Cup World Champion Doubles Team; Ham Richardson, a Davis Cup player who was No. 1 in the United States in the 1950s; and Bob McKinley, the National Indoor 18-and-Under Champion. Slew Hestor of Jackson, Mississippi – a U.S. Lawn Tennis Association (USLTA) officer – and Alfred Alschuler, Chair of the Facilities Committee of USLTA, were also introduced.

Sunday's events included an open house for members and friends and a tennis exhibition in the afternoon followed by a dinner that was attended by 860 people.

March 7, 1969,
The Honorable
George H.W. Bush,
speaking when he was
U.S. Representative Bush at
the HRC Grand Opening Gala

March 9, 1969,
HRC fans watching an
exhibition tennis match

THE PRECEDING YEARS
As told by Tom Eaton – HRC charter member who joined in 1966

For everything that takes place, there are always the preceding events that foretell and/or make the events that follow successful. Such was the case with HRC.

What occurred was the collateral effect of a few teenage Houstonians who went into the military in the final years of World War II. There, they became used to going to the enlisted men's club, the NCO Club, or the Officer's Club where one could buy a drink and a steak.

However, upon returning to civilian life and finishing college, they realized that such privileges did not exist in Houston. Texas was a "brown bag" state, which meant you couldn't buy a drink, a bottle, or even a glass of wine in a restaurant.

So a few inventive and ambitious souls decided the answer was to form a private club that would be affordable for a young, out-of-college male with a limited income and a big vision. Curly Lewis and Tyne Sparks created a plan in which 20 young men each put up $200 and chartered a private club in the spring of 1951. It was christened The Key Club for one simple reason: There were not enough members to create sufficient cash flow to afford a location and a staff, so each member had a key to get in.

The original location was Tyne Sparks' parents' garage apartment. But with the original $4,000 and a few new members, No. 2 Chelsea Place was purchased, and the club had a stand-alone location. A few years later, land on Sage Road (between San Felipe and Westheimer) was purchased from the family of one of the charter members, and a real clubhouse with a swimming pool and a few tennis courts was built.

By the mid-1950s, the membership had increased to the point that there were sufficient funds available to hire a full-time manager and establish regular hours so that the keys were no longer necessary. With that, a new name was chosen, motivated by the location on Sage Road: The Sagewood Country Club.

But when the 1960s rolled around, Sagewood's future had become cloudy. Some members wanted to sell the property; others wanted to add a golf course; still others were committed to preserving a tennis-only club. But one thing was certain: A change was going to come.

And it did, in the form of oilman George Mitchell, who was already on a mission to create a major tennis club in Houston. Never one to let an opportunity pass, Mitchell saw the potential that a merger with Sagewood held. He knew that liquidating the Sage Road property – and bringing as many of the club's members as possible to a new facility – would generate the kind of money needed to get his dream off the ground.

Mitchell's plan paid off. He arranged the sale of Sagewood for $338,000, enabling the purchase of 26 acres off Memorial Drive where a top-tier club could be built to serve a membership that had suddenly jumped from 400 to 750. The Houston Racquet Club had a new home.

HOUSTON RACQUET CLUB

A PROPOSED PRIVATE CLUB
FOR THE PURPOSE OF DEVELOPING AND
ENJOYING TENNIS, SWIMMING AND SOCIAL
ACTIVITIES FOR THE ENTIRE FAMILY

LUDUS PRO FAMILIA CUNCTA

MEMBERSHIP DETAILS

HOUSTON RACQUET CLUB:

• 1965-1967: 400 founding and charter Houston Racquet Club members paid an initiation fee of $600-$800

• September 1965: During the first month, individuals could put down $100 as a deposit in the HRC escrow account signaling their intent to join

• Monthly dues of $20-$25 included a $2 monthly fee per member that was donated to what is now known as the Houston Tennis Association

SAGEWOOD COUNTRY CLUB :

• 1965-1967: Original Sagewood Country Club membership initiation fee was $240

• May 5, 1966: The merger of HRC and Sagewood was officially filed with the Secretary of State of the State of Texas and was signed by James A. Walsh, representing HRC, and Joel Howard Smith, representing Sagewood

• 360 Sagewood members joined with HRC

• Sagewood members got an $800 credit to be applied to their members' accounts for use against dues, bar bills, or food

• The originial meetings between HRC members and Sagewood members took place at the Houston Country Club

"LUDUS PRO FAMILIA CUNCTA"

This Latin phrase, which means "Sport for the Whole Family," is found on the cover of the original HRC marketing brochure from 1965. The Club is still using the motto today as it exemplifies what HRC is all about.

▲▶
March 7, 1969,
Photos from the
HRC Grand
Opening Gala

In the name and by the authority of

The State of Texas

OFFICE OF THE SECRETARY OF STATE

CERTIFICATE OF INCORPORATION

OF

HOUSTON RACQUET CLUB
Charter No. 217473

The undersigned, as Secretary of State of the State of Texas, hereby certifies that duplicate originals of Articles of Incorporation for the above corporation duly signed and verified pursuant to the provisions of the Texas Non-Profit Corporation Act, have been received in this office and are found to conform to law.

ACCORDINGLY the undersigned, as such Secretary of State, and by virtue of the authority vested in him by law, hereby issues this Certificate of Incorporation and attaches hereto a duplicate original of the Articles of Incorporation.

Dated October 1st , 1965.

Secretary of State

◄

1965, Original HRC
Certificate of Incorporation

▶

1968, HRC
construction photos

March 9, 1969,
HRC Grand
Opening weekend

HOUSTON RACQUET CLUB
10709 MEMORIAL DRIVE HOUSTON
TEXAS 77024

ESTABLISHED 1966

August 7, 1967

Dear Fellow Club Member:

Traditionally, no club news bulletin is published for the month of August. But, we have work under way at our Memorial Drive site - the first project of our construction program; that's good news to all of us who've been none-too-patiently waiting. With Mr. Walsh vacationing in the City by the Bay, it's up to me to spread the word. This concerns our first six tennis courts, which we had hoped to have completed a month ago.

The thing that held us up on those was what you might call "political."

JOEL H. SMITH, HRC FIRST VICE PRESIDENT, FOUNDING MEMBER
Excerpt from a letter to the membership dated August 7, 1967

You know . . . sometimes in the rush of phone calls, meetings, resolutions, contracts, deadlines, etc., you can lose track of the significance of basic things. The other day I walked back to the far-end of the clearing at the Club site, and I was struck again by the incredible beauty of this place. With the bayou at my back, I could barely glimpse the traffic far away on Memorial Drive - is it really half a mile? It's so huge! Even after we finish all phases of our building program, more than a third of it will remain in it's natural state, a legacy of space for our future . . . My six years of service at Sagewood and the Racquet Club are drawing to a close. What began - for me - long ago with plans for a children's party now ends with an undreamed-of promise for the future; a sports club of national stature. Incredible.

Yours sincerely,

Joel

Joel H. Smith
First Vice President

CHAPTER TWO

AN HRC HOME AND CHANGES
THROUGH THE YEARS

HIS DREAM WOULD NOT HAVE BECOME THE REALITY IT IS TODAY WITHOUT THE VISION OF KARL KAMRATH.

March 9, 1969,
HRC Grand Opening
exhibition tennis match

WHILE GEORGE MITCHELL WAS THE UNDENIABLE FORCE BEHIND THE DEVELOPMENT OF THE HOUSTON RACQUET CLUB, HIS DREAM WOULD NOT HAVE BECOME THE REALITY IT IS TODAY WITHOUT THE VISION OF KARL KAMRATH.

A renowned architect and devotee of Frank Lloyd Wright, Kamrath had the creative insight to design a club on a unique piece of property that would have long-lasting value.

And there were tests – some structural, others natural.

After the initial construction of the Clubhouse and courts, the Club was confronted with growing pains that led to new additions, remodeling, and the need to consider more mergers. But finally, after decades of somewhat modest changes, HRC came into the 21st century with a renovated look and feel that was built around the Fitness Center, resort pools, and Pavilion.

But Mother Nature posed challenges as well. The Club has survived hurricanes and floods, in every case coming back better than ever and demonstrating the kind of goodwill, strength, and character that has defined HRC throughout its 50-year history.

KARL KAMRATH SR.
HRC ARCHITECT

Karl Kamrath was born April 25, 1911, in Enid, Oklahoma, but spent his boyhood in Austin and then attended the University of Texas. He was a competitive tennis player, winning the NCAA Doubles Championship in 1931 and U.S. Lawn Tennis Association Father-and-Son Championship in 1952. Kamrath turned down the chance to play tennis professionally and instead moved to Chicago to work as an architect. During World War II, he served as a captain in the United States Army Corps of Engineers. After leaving the service, he and fellow UT graduate Fred MacKie opened their Houston architectural firm, MacKie and Kamrath.

In June 1946, Kamrath had the opportunity to meet Frank Lloyd Wright and they became close friends. Kamrath believed in what Wright called Usonian principles – the idea that architecture has an inherent relationship with both its site and its time. HRC's architecture is considered to be in the manner of Frank Lloyd Wright's work, and Kamrath designed many Houston buildings that bear his signature style, including Memorial Drive Presbyterian Church, St. John the Divine Episcopal Church, and many houses in the River Oaks and Memorial areas.

He was married to Jeanie Sampson, an active tennis player and teaching pro in Houston, and they had four children before divorcing in 1975. He died in Houston in January 1988. The Kamrath Collection, which includes his correspondence and notes with Frank Lloyd Wright, is housed at The University of Texas at Austin School of Architecture.

MERGING A USONIAN TENNIS VIEW

"Building the Club in today's environment would present a plethora of barriers that were not considered in the mid-1960s. Regulations didn't oversee land development, EPA issues, disruption of 'natural habitats,' etc. Our beautiful Club is the result, on time and under budget."

"Karl was a good tennis player. He played in the 1931 River Oaks tournament and many others around the country. Those days there wasn't prize money – just the love of the game and competition."

- Jeanie Kamrath Gonzales –
HRC Architect Karl Kamrath's former wife, now 104 years old

HRC Architect
Karl Kamrath Sr.

natural setting so as to become integrated with the sloping ground. The whole design will achieve a friendly and informal atmosphere.

■ The main level will contain a large entrance portecochere, a story and a half lobby controlled by the club receptionist next to the administrative offices of the club manager. A large flexible lounge area with a card room adjoins the lobby and features an intimate inglenook several steps below the lounge level built around a fireplace. The lounge opens onto a large shaded open terrace that will immediately overlook three feature tennis courts at a lower level. From the upper terrace, access is provided to the swimming area at a still lower ravine level.

■ Up a half-flight from the lobby is the main ballroom, cocktail lounge and dining areas. A feature of the ballroom is a long glassed-in balcony that overlooks a beautiful terraced ravine and several nearby tennis courts. The cocktail lounge will look down into the entrance lobby and will have

direct access to the 3 private dining rooms and appropriate restro__ large efficient kitchen will serve the private dining rooms, cocktail l__ main dining room with fireplace, the main ballroom and glazed ba__ The ballroom features a multi-level ceiling and orchestra shell and __ signed to be divided in order to accommodate several different __ functions.

■ Down from the lobby a half-flight will be the mixed grille, bar, __ locker and shower rooms with exercise, sauna bath and massage ro__

■ The tennis professional office is at one end of the men's locker r__ and will overlook the entire tennis activities for proper supervision. __ on this level will be the ladies' card room, locker room, sauna, exer__ and massage rooms adjoining their shower room featuring private dres__ areas. Carpeted floors will be used in both locker rooms.

■ The mixed grille and bar and men's locker rooms will open dire__

THE VISION OF HRC
1967 HRC Marketing Brochure

An HRC promotional brochure included Kamrath's architectural vision of the Club building. His goal was to capture Frank Lloyd Wright's Usonian principles:

"Construction materials will be masonry, rough-hewn stained wood, and stained and plate glass. The architecture will be organic in character to comply to and blend with the natural setting so as to become integrated with the sloping ground. The whole design will achieve a friendly and informal atmosphere...

"Because of the undulating wooded site, the architects have taken advantage of this rolling natural terrain to the extent that outdoor activities will be located on various levels with terraces which will add greatly to the visual interest of the landscaped layout...

"Long range plans call for some of the courts to be enclosed and air conditioned. Also included in long range plans will be a tennis stadium built around two championship courts, and the entire tennis layout can be effectively used to conduct tournaments and exhibitions of national and international importance."

1973, Ruthe Wilson and Trina
Knipe looking at plans to
decorate the cocktail lounge

ORIGINAL CONSTRUCTION FINANCING

1966-1967: The overall annual operating budget for the merged HRC and Sagewood Country Club was $1.5 million.

While construction of the first six courts was underway, members used the Sage Road property (Sagewood) for social activities. For a short period of time, dues were adjusted to allow for the temporary "two-campus" arrangement.

FINANCING CAME FROM THREE SOURCES:

- Membership escrow accounts
- Credits from the transfer and sale of the Sage Road property
- Mortgage financing

1967: Swimming pool and 18 tennis courts opened in the summer

1969: Clubhouse and balance of facilities opened

HRC'S 1967-1969 CONSTRUCTION TEAM:

Architects – MacKie and Kamrath, A.I.A.

General Contractor – T.D. Howe Construction Company

Mechanical Engineering – Fred Holste

Structural Engineering – Walter Moore

Landscaping – Bishop and Walker

Night Lighting – John Watson

Interior Design – Evans-Monical

THE SHACK
As told by Jim Bayless – A "member from literally day one" and a self-described "Fossil of the Piney Woods"

Then-HRC head pro Richard Nesmith, son of Bob Nesmith, the forever head pro at Memorial Park Tennis Center, hired me (age 15 at the time) in the summer of 1967 to open up the "tennis shop" (shed/trailer) on Sunday mornings at eight. I first had to buy a few wooden crates of Nehi strawberry soda and root beer and Cokes at the Texaco station on Voss and San Felipe.

The trip to the courts was a pilgrimage: Turn off Memorial Drive into the woods and drive along a meandering dirt "driveway" deep into the forest, past where that residence is (or was). Eventually, you arrived at four Laykold courts. The "regular" who never missed a Sunday doubles match was a gentleman named Alex Pegues (pa-GEEZ). Other early members were longtime patrons of Memorial Park T.C., including among others, Ronnie Fisher, Richard Schuette, and John Been. I answered the phone in the primitive trailer, booked court reservations, and otherwise entertained the (few) members as they arrived. I had the whole place to myself the entire summer and enjoyed the peace and quiet.

Only years later was any headway made on the Clubhouse. Then the timber flew, as pine trees galore came a-toppling to make way for a gazillion courts, overwhelmingly Har-Tru.

▲
1969, Jack Kamrath and Jim Bayless on the HRC courts

THE RACONTEUR

JUNE   1970

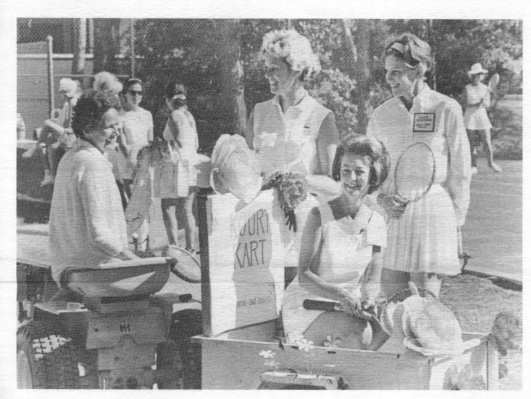

These women dominated Betty Ewing's Society Column in the Chronicle. Operating the refreshment "Kourt Kart" were Marion Weyrauch, chairman, Nelle Patton, Dorothy Schleider, and Ellen Koehler.

Member-Guest Tournament Draws Record Participation

Four sets of winners emerged from the member-guest tournament at HRC May 5 and 6. Championship flight winners were **Mrs. Richard E. Schuette** and her guest, **Mrs. Peter Pratt**, who defeated **Mrs. Robert H. Washington** and her guest, **Mrs. W. A. Whitfill**, 6-4, 705. In first flight competition, **Mrs. Jeff Dyke** and her guest, **Mrs. David Chapman**, defeated **Mrs. Ben T. Withers, Jr.**, and her guest, **Mrs. Howard R. Gould**, 603, 6-1.

Entries totaled 180 women.

In the second flight, winners were **Mrs. Paul D. Garvey** and her guest, **Mrs. Wm. A. Smith**, who defeated **Mrs. Carl R. Apthorp III** and her guest, **Mrs. Brooks Hamilton**, 6-4, 3-6, 6-3. Winners of the third flight were **Mrs. Taylor Durham** and her guest, **Mrs. Don Donnelly**, who defeated **Mrs. Louis K. Brandt**, and her guest, **Mrs. Paul Christian**, 6-4, 8-6.

HRC Pro Proves He's a Top Player

Big news in tennis competition was Jerry Evert's win in the 45-and-over singles at the River Oaks tournament in April. He beat Bob Kamrath. Evert and Dick Rogers who got to the quarter finals in doubles at River Oaks were beaten by Bob Kamrath and Rennie Baker, who then played (and lost) in the semi-finals.

Another member, Jack Jackson, competed in the ___ournament until he was defeated by the fourth-___eeded player in the third round. Jackson had ___eviously defeated Mike Estep, who is nationally ___ked.

___ther tournament winners were as follows:
___dies Day, April 21: winners, Hodgson & Van ___; runners-up — Brandt & Rozelle.
___es Day, May 12: winners, Ellis & Thompson; ___. & Nommensen; runners-up — Brandt &

___ Doubles: winners — Mrs. Earl Ricks' &
___ane; Mrs. and Mrs. Robert Beamon; Mr.
___ David Cornell; Mr. and Mrs. Arthur Bell;
___. Hugh McGee.
___azy Mixed-up Doubles, April 28: winners
___shington & Ruth Wilson; Audra Cox &
___g; Norma Boyle & Jane Peacock; Ellen
___ Betty Ellis; Jackie Kahn & Elaine
___ Ladies Day, March 24, Bell &
___ the winners.

___ Match
___sday Night

___eld during the summer will be
___ at 5:15 p.m. ___eks with mixed doubles
___32 teams,

___oint accumu-
___nts will again
___ to play at 10

___bles, is
___is divi-
___ough
___xtra
___w.

HRC Hires Schmoeller As New Assistant Pro

Gary Schmoeller, most recently from Fort Worth, is the new tennis pro at HRC.

Gary received his B.B.A. from the University of Texas at El Paso in 1967 with an emphasis on economics and marketing. After college, he served in the U. S. Army at Fort Lewis, Wash., where he organized and conducted a tennis program for the Special Services Division. He played number one position for the Fort Lewis Tennis Team and travelled the West Coast competing in tournament play in California, Oregon, Washington, and British Columbia.

Prior to that he played in the number one position for UT at El Paso and assisted the club pro at the El Paso Tennis Club with instructions and stringing rackets.

He achieved a ranking of number 11 in Texas in junior ranking. His college play was in Texas, Arizona, New Mexico, and Colorado.

Sparkle Plenty on July 4

The Racquet Club will don red, white, and blue Saturday, July 4. Balloons, clowns, ice cream, soft drinks, and pony rides for the children and a barbecue dinner and an oompah band for everyone ___ill make the occasion festive. ___lan to celebrate the fourth at HRC.

Social:

Belmont Day is June 6. It's another chance to enjoy the races in the cool comfort of HRC. This includes Make reservations for $5 a person. This includes the racing entertainment, a luncheon from 1:30 to 2:30 p.m., music by Russell Jackson's band from 2 to 6, and the race at 4:30. Cocktails are first served at noon. Stay for dinner, which is optional.

★ ★ ★

Games nights return to Thursday, June 4 and 18. Buffet dinner beforehand and two game cards cost $5, and dinner is served from 6:30 to 8 p.m. Games begin immediately after, and game cards (without the dinner) cost $1.

★ ★ ★

Special Thursdays are set for June 11 and 25. Drinks are served (in the ballroom and main bar only) for 60 cents each. A buffet is served from 7 to ___ p.m. for $3. Make reservations.

★ ★ ★

___ day June

Sport:

A tournament for junior players will begin on June 5. It will be a round robin where each player plays all others in his age division. It will extend through June 12. A challenge ladder will be formed for the summer from the results.

Divisions included are boys, 10, 12, 14, 16, and 18 and under. Girls divisions are 12, 14, 16, and 18 and under. Each participant must play in his own age division, but the best four in each will be allowed to challenge in a higher division.

Tennis age is determined by the birthday in 1970, even if it is as late as December.

★ ★ ★

The **pool** opens full time in June. Fred Breck-woldt and Jan Hansel are teaching again this year. Call 464-5003 for swimming lesson reservations.

★ ★ ★

___ still enroll in the sportarama sessions ___ 1 are eligible for the two ___ 24. Sign up

▲

Early HRC *Raconteur*
newsletters

THE HOWE HOUSE

T.D. Howe grew up in Boston, Massachusetts, and received his undergraduate and master's degrees in civil engineering from Harvard and MIT, respectively. He went into the construction business with his father, who sent him to Houston to work on a project for him. It didn't take long before T.D. Howe fell in love with the city and moved his wife here, telling her: "There's not horses and cattle everywhere like you've heard about." Their first home was near the Club in the 9000 block of Memorial.

When Mrs. Howe was pregnant with their fourth child, she told her husband it was time for a bigger house. Hence… the Howe House was built on the property where HRC now stands. In the early 1960s, T.D. Howe sold the front acreage to George Butler, who eventually made a deal with George Mitchell to buy the land.

The Howe family stayed in their home and on the remaining six acres. A few years later, HRC began the competitive bidding process for the new Clubhouse, and T.D. Howe was determined to win the job, which he did. His oldest son, Dike, recounted, "My father said he has to be the lowest bid because he would not be too happy waking up every morning to a competitor building the Clubhouse on his old property right in front of the house!"

In the early 1970s, all the Howe children were grown and living elsewhere. The Howes decided the home was too big for just the two of them, and none of their children were interested in buying it. So in 1972, a deal was struck with HRC to purchase the house and acreage, and the rest – as they say – is history.

The Howe House is now used for storage and its bathroom is available to players on the nearby tennis courts.

◄

The Howe House in
the early 1970s

Mid-1980s,
Aerial photo of HRC

ANOTHER POSSIBLE MERGER?

During 1985-1986, discussions with Memorial Drive Country Club (off Voss Road between Woodway and Memorial Drive) were initiated to see if merging the clubs was a good idea. After appraisals were completed and came back lower than anticipated – along with flood plain issues related to Buffalo Bayou – HRC decided against it. Memorial Drive Country Club closed, and the property was sold and distributed to its members – many of whom would actually join HRC in the coming months.

Houston Racquet Club
Swim Team 2003

2003, HRC swim team

In 1988, the Board began researching adding a Fitness Center to HRC. The decision was made to add a facility with weights and cardio equipment adjacent to the pool deck and near the locker rooms in the Clubhouse.

"In the late 1980s, there was massive opposition to spending money for the original Fitness Center, particularly from the older members. The Board went ahead and built one, in the area that's now the children's center. After people got used to the facility, the older members became the biggest users, showing you can teach old dogs."
- Horst Manhard – HRC General Manager
1977-2005

Mid-1990s,
Fitness Center

◄ ►
2005, construction underway on the resort pools and Pavilion

2000-2003 NEW CLUBHOUSE DISCUSSIONS

After 35+ years, HRC began to show some wear and tear. In early 2001, the Long Range Planning Committee performed a study on the Clubhouse and presented options to continue with the existing building or plan for a new building at some point in the future. In the end, after much debate, the Club overwhelmingly voted to keep the current building and renovate as need be in the future. In just a few short years, the Club began work on its next major project, the addition of the Fitness Center, Pavilion and resort pools.

2003-2006 HRC RESORT POOLS, PAVILION, AND FITNESS CENTER CONSTRUCTION

PHASE I

JUNE 2003 – Plans for the project began focusing on expanding Club amenities.
JULY 2004 – Phase I improvements were underway and included renovation of the ballroom and expansion of the Club's casual dining grill and bar area overlooking Soldiers Creek.

PHASE II

MARCH 2005 – Groundbreaking was celebrated for the $4.5 million Phase II pool complex, which included a resort-style pool with water fountains and a graduated beach entry as well as a children's play area. The new construction included an Olympic-sized, heated lap pool; poolside baths and changing areas; a covered Pavilion with outdoor fireplace and bar area; a new café; a 2,000-square-foot teen activity center; an on-site daycare center; and a sand volleyball and basketball area. Part of Phase II was the gated entry from Memorial Drive that also housed the Memorial Villages Police Department substation.

PHASE III

JUNE 2005 – Phase III of the project was underway and included the "crown jewel" – the $5 million Fitness Center, which featured a large exercise area with weight training and cardio exercise equipment; specialized rooms for yoga, aerobics, and Pilates; Pilates Reformer machines; and men's and ladies' locker rooms. The center, constructed with Texas limestone and exposed beams, provides expansive views of the lush wooded area along Soldiers Creek.

2004-2005,
Construction
underway on the
new resort pools,
Fitness Center,
parking area and
Pavilion

March 2006,
Completed HRC
resort pools,
Pavilion and
Fitness Center

GRAND OPENING

During the weekend of May 28-29, 2006, the Club celebrated the unveiling of its $12 million three-phase project to renovate and expand its facilities, including resort-style pools, a Fitness Center with state-of-the-art equipment, and new dining options with a café and Pavilion. More than 700 members attended the festivities, which included a ribbon cutting ceremony for the new buildings and a presentation of special sculptures to honor the past founders of the Club. Recognized at the event were past founding members Kenneth Burroughs, Hugh McGee Jr., Toni Duperier (daughter of the late founder James Walsh), and Jeanie Kamrath Gonzalez, former wife of Club architect Karl Kamrath Sr. Twenty past Club presidents were also in attendance.

October 2008   HOUSTON RACQUET CLUB

RACONTEUR
Events of Interest

Ike's Grand Slam!

www.houstonracquetclub.com

◀

October 2008, HRC
Raconteur newsletter cover

▶

2008, Hurricane Ike
damage being surveyed by
2007-2008 Club President
Bob Landauer

2005 HURRICANE KATRINA

As a gesture of goodwill and friendship, HRC offered temporary reciprocal memberships to any member who had evacuated here from the New Orleans Lawn Tennis Club after Hurricane Katrina. About 40 New Orleans evacuees joined HRC while their homes were renovated and repaired – and some even stayed in Houston and remain members today.

2008 HURRICANE IKE

On September 10, 2008, HRC General Manager Thomas Preuml, CCM, who had been on the job only two days, called Club President Bob Landauer to ask for approval to shut the Club down. Hurricane Ike was headed on a course to Houston. The Club "battened down the hatches" and hoped for the best. The storm hit on September 13 and caused massive damage throughout the Memorial Villages area, with trees down and debris littering the streets. HRC was without power for 15 days and the Clubhouse remained closed, but 48 hours after the storm left, the staff managed to get 20 courts clean and playable. Only the Fitness Center, Howe House, and maintenance building had roof and water damage.

A POWER WAITING GAME

"Remember the power company's zip code map, outlining estimated electricity restoration dates? I kept staring at 77024, waiting for that promising light blue color, which stood for 'back to civilization.' My makeshift office during this time was the Courtside Café patio, and when we finally opened the Clubhouse again on September 30, my first month at the Club was already over."

-Thomas Preuml, CCM – HRC General Manager and COO

SOLDIERS CREEK EROSION

In April 2009, Houston had a torrential rainstorm that flooded the city. At the back of HRC's property, Buffalo Bayou filled to capacity, and the water in Soldiers Creek came upstream instead of flowing downstream. Then, just like an ocean wave at the shoreline, the water retreated and took the sides of Soldiers Creek with it.

The Fitness Center and pool complex were literally within a few feet of falling into the creek. Water covered the Club's foundation pillars and came up to the office entrance on the east side. The embankment then softened, causing the main sewer drain located behind the resort pool fence to detach from the pipe draining water into Soldiers Creek.

The Club reacted swiftly and effectively, putting into place a three-phase plan to repair the damage. Phase I started right after the flooding and consisted of cleaning up; removing the trees and shrubs from the two fallout areas at the Fitness Center and resort pool area; and covering the erosion sites with tarps to prevent further damage. Phase II began in the summer of 2009 and included rerouting Soldiers Creek away from the Clubhouse and creating a runoff drain to capture water from the roof, embankment, and parking lots. In Phase III, which began during the winter of 2010, the two fallout areas were filled with concrete blocks and approximately 100 30-foot steel beams to further stabilize the embankments.

The Club worked closely with the Harris County Flood Control District and the Hunters Creek city engineer to develop a plan that would benefit both HRC and the community by preventing further flooding problems. The final cost to repair the erosion was around $1.2 million and was completed in 2012.

▶

April 2009,
Flood damage

2009-2012, Soldiers Creek
erosion reconstruction
and repair

CHAPTER THREE
**TENNIS – A CHAPTER OF
HRC ACCOMPLISHMENTS**

HE DREAMED OF CREATING A TENNIS
CLUB THAT WOULD BE CELEBRATED
AS ONE OF THE BEST IN THE COUNTRY.

1973, HRC players: Front LtoR, Keri Soifer, Rhonda Tomasco, Don Tomasco;
Center LtoR, Paul Garvey, Jay Iler, Charles Sullivan;
Back LtoR, Shelly Stolaroff, Mary Stevens, David Iler

1974, Nick Stephens

FROM THE BEGINNING, GEORGE MITCHELL
IMAGINED THE HOUSTON RACQUET CLUB
AS MORE THAN JUST A DOZEN OR SO
TENNIS COURTS AND A CLUBHOUSE. Rather,
he dreamed of creating a tennis club that would be celebrated as one of
the best in the country. But there weren't a lot of blueprints for his vision,
as only a handful of clubs nationwide at the time were focused on tennis;
most were dedicated to golf.

Mitchell's idea was somewhat revolutionary and required finding like-
minded members who also wanted HRC to be something special. He knew
where to locate these local tennis players, and most of them joined without
hesitation. It was the start of a unique, novel idea for a club – based on
the sport of tennis but well rounded enough to attract other members
whose passion did not necessarily involve a net, a racquet, and a white
or yellow ball.

But like most of Mitchell's ideas, it paid off, and in just a few short
years, HRC had attracted some of the best players in the world as
members. Not long after that, top-ranked pros joined the Club to teach.
The Texas oilman's dream had become a reality: top players, top pros, a
waiting list for membership, a beautiful Clubhouse, and an impressive 26
tennis courts on which to play.

It didn't stop there, though. Now that HRC's national reputation
was building, the next milestone was to get the same recognition from
the international tennis world. And the Club found an unexpected – and
unprecedented – path to that acclaim in the early 1970s, when it was at the
forefront of the most important battle in women's tennis: the start of the
controversial Professional Women's Tour, which began at HRC. The Club
would later go on to become host of the National Senior Women's Clay
Court Championships.

Other landmark tennis events would take place over the next 50 years,
solidifying HRC's place as one of the most important tennis clubs in the
country, whose impact and reach has been worldwide.

February 5, 2015

Dear HRC Members,

The city of Houston and specifically the Houston Racquet Club have long played a vital role in the growth of tennis in this country. Both the club and the city will forever be linked to the birth of women's professional tennis as we know it today and I could not be happier to congratulate you on your anniversary!

In September 1970 when the Original 9 signed $1 contracts with Gladys Heldman to play in the Virginia Slims of Houston, we did so at Gladys' home just around the corner from your Club. When we played the first ever Virginia Slims tournament, we did so at your Club.

We could not have done it without the support and the blood, sweat and tears of your membership. Delores Hornberger and the Women's Association of the Houston Racquet Club led the charge and raised the prize money and got the tournament properly organized. Without the help of people like Delores, Leslie Creekmore, Sybil Stephens, Nelle Patton and Charlotte Lorenz, the tournament may never have happened.

George Mitchell, one of the founders of your club, became Delores' guardian angel and played a major behind-the-scenes role in the birth of women's professional tennis.

From our beginnings here at the Houston Racquet Club, the WTA Tour has grown to include 2,500 players representing 92 nations competing in 55 events in 33 countries offering more than $258 million in prize money.

Yes, we have come a long way and every woman who ever made or currently makes a living playing professional tennis owes a great deal to The Houston Racquet Club. We can't thank you enough for all you have done. You are indeed a game changer.

Congratulations!

Billie Jean King

THE RACONTE
NOVEMBER

President's Ball

Glitter and glamour settle on HRC November 7, the night of the President's Ball. The formal affair begins at 7 p.m. with cocktails, dinner at 8, and dancing to Bob Smith's Orchestra from 8 until midnight. The $25 fee per couple includes dinner, music, and beverages.

Open tables will be set up for members who want to meet other members. Please make reservations.

The new president and the new board of directors will be introduced at the ball.

Talent S
Early V
For Sta

The HRC
stage produ
out the ca
set for the
interested
let her k
The t
Billing
season
Brow
appe
Inc
"W
"C
d

-- PHOTO BY BILL

Dan Lovett interviews Billie Jean King on
day of the Virginia Slims Invitational for Ch

Joe Garagiola
called it

Question: King or Riggs?

Billie Jean King

Bobby Riggs

vs. female contest, though. It's very interesting and will do a lot for tennis by putting it before the public—that is, if it's not promoted like a boxing or wrestling match, in an unsophisticated way . . ."

Mary Keegan wants Billie Jean t
"I'm glad they held out for
The purses should
prayers are f

R 1970

matter who wins on the court, the
f the most barbs will remain for-
s-up. Billie Jean King and Bobby
varming up for their September
e match with a volley of well-
fast backhanded remarks,
aneuvering for the advant-

is such a ready topic,
members of the club
reaction to and pre-

t as an interesting
perience against
k Bobby Riggs
to see him
is as a male

ts Seek nteers Production

s Association's second annual
high-strung players is sending
ent! December 4 at 7:30 p.m. is
reading and discussion for all
Delores Hornberger, 782-2567, and
can attend.

cting talent of Chuck and Sherry
ready been snared. The two are
ston actors. Mr. Billing, who is with
oby, Inc., an advertising agency, has
the shows he has appeared in are
g Town," "Visit to a Small Planet" and
ul House." Mrs. Billing, a speech and
the House. Mrs. Billing, taught speech at Spring
major in college, until she moved into adminis-
l High School, until she moved into adminis-
work. For two summers in a row, the Billings
cted the summer drama festival at the YWCA.
sorts of talent are needed -- actors, actresses,
ers, dancers, prop girls, lighting, set manager,
ge manager, make-up, entre acts, etc. Last year's "Show-
tions, make-up, entre acts, etc. Last year's "Show-
oat" was a roaring success, and the participants
had a marvelous time entertaining.
Don't miss the December 4 meeting -- the first,
and it is hoped, the last call for talent. On January
8, casting will begin. Meetings are also set for March
19 and 20.

Joan Reid

HRC

A buffe
King-Riggs
proceed to t
The 5 p.m.
ride costs $8

Men's Challenge Doubles Set

A men's challenge doubles tournament will begin
November 1. It is open to all but championship.
Sign up at $4 per team. Complete details are posted
in the pro shop. The event will be concluded the
first of February.

-- PHOTO BY BELA UGRIN, HOUSTON POST

The proud pros hold high their new contract money. Front row, l to r, are Judy Tegart Dalton, Kerry Melville, Rosemary Casals, World Tennis publisher Gladys Heldman, and Kristy Pigeon. Back row, l to r, are Valerie Ziegenfuss, Billie Jean King, Nancy Richey, and Peaches Bartkowicz.

Tennis World Eyes Action At Virginia Slims Invitational

Tennis history was made last September when nine of the top women tennis players in the world competed in the $5,000 Virginia Slims Invitational tennis tournament in September at HRC. The event, sponsored by the Women's Association of HRC, was just an "ordinary" top-notch attraction until the women announced -- only 30 minutes before the tournament -- that they had signed as contract pros with **World Tennis**, published by new Houston resident, Gladys Heldman. Then it rocked the tennis world.

Billie Jean King, Rosemary Casals, Judy Tegart Dalton, Nancy Richey, Kerry Melville, Valerie Ziegenfuss, Kristy Pigeon, and Peaches Bartkowicz accepted $1 bill to signify their new status. Only Patti Hogan, who was committed to a series of tournaments in England, declined to sign. Instead, she played in the doubles events.

Continued on page 6

THE NET SET

The Fabulous New Houston Racquet Club

50¢

Apr. '69

▶
April 1969,
Christine Muller
posing for the
cover of *The Net Set*
magazine

HRC – THE OFFICIAL SITE OF THE WOMEN'S PROFESSIONAL TOUR

They hadn't come a long way quite yet.

It was 1970, and male professional tennis players were making over $100,000 in a season. The same, however, could not be said of women; in some cases, men were earning 12 times what their female counterparts were being paid for a single tournament. There was just a prevailing belief that men deserved more because fans would pay to watch them – but not women – play.

Angry at the economic disparity, a group of women players led by Billie Jean King contacted Gladys Heldman, the founder of *World Tennis* magazine and an HRC member. They said they wanted to boycott a major U.S. Lawn Tennis Association (USLTA) event in protest. But Heldman had a better idea:

Hold a women's professional event that same weekend in Houston at the Club.

The USLTA was not happy and threatened to suspend any woman who entered. But Heldman was undeterred and came up with a plan that bordered on genius. She signed nine players – known as the "Original 9" – who were willing to take on the USLTA to a "personal services" contract with her magazine for $1 apiece: King, Rosemary Casals, Nancy Richey, Peaches Bartkowicz, Kristy Pigeon, Valerie Ziegenfuss, Julie Heldman, Kerry Melville, and Judy Tegart Dalton. Those agreements technically made the Houston event a professional tournament and removed it from the USLTA's authority. However, the USLTA was steadfast in its opposition and suspended them all anyway. But at that point, it didn't matter. Gladys Heldman had secured a $7,500 purse – including a critical financial commitment from HRC founder George Mitchell; had a terrific venue in the HRC; and had attracted some of the best players in the world to appear in the Houston Women's Invitational. Beyond that, she had locked down the support of Joe Cullman, Chairman of the Board of Philip Morris, who had donated $2,500 for the right to brand the tournament as the Virginia Slims Invitational.

Even though the USLTA said it would not sanction the event, the matches went on anyway (although Billie Jean King had to retire after a single point due to a knee injury). Casals won, defeating Dalton 5-7, 6-1, 7-5.

By the end of 1970, the small band of nine tennis "revolutionaries" had grown to 40. The Houston event spawned eight additional professional tournaments sponsored by Virginia Slims. And by 1973, the Virginia Slims Circuit would become the Women's Tennis Association.

◄

1970, Gladys Heldman talking to Charles Carder of the *Houston Chronicle*

▶

1970, Gladys Heldman welcoming fans to HRC at the first Virginia Slims Women's Tour, with Jim Hight (Tournament Director) to her left, and Delores Hornberger to her right

▼

Gladys Heldman through the years

GLADYS HELDMAN:
A DAUGHTER'S PERSPECTIVE

(Excerpts from a speech Julie Heldman gave accepting the Georgina Clark Mother Award from the Women's Tennis Association (WTA) on behalf of her late mother, Gladys Heldman, in April 2012. Gladys Heldman was a member of HRC and considered the founder of the Women's Professional Tennis Tour, which was launched at HRC in 1970.)

This award is certainly not because Gladys Heldman was a traditional mother. She was unapologetically unconventional. She didn't cook, she didn't clean, she didn't vacuum. She was uninterested in makeup and frilly dresses. But she was a helluva role model. She taught us to value education and success, she was committed to helping others, and she stood up for what she believed in.

She was extraordinarily hard working. She graduated from Stanford in three years, at the top of her class. In 1953, she started, owned, edited, and published *World Tennis*, which became the world's largest and most influential tennis magazine. When she sold the magazine in 1972, she liked to say she was replaced by seven men. That's probably true.

She was dedicated to helping tennis players. Without any publicity, she paid for players who couldn't afford to compete. At a time when opportunities were few for players of color, she reached out a hand to those in need. All of these traits came in handy when she founded the women's pro tour.

Her creativity as a promoter led to a unique solution. In 1970, the rules distinguishing amateurs and pros were complex. To make the tournament work, my mother creatively made all the players contract pros for one week by signing them up for $1. That solution protected the players and the Club.

Her connection to Joe Cullman was vital. She called him and got Virginia Slims, his company's new women's brand, to support the tournament.

Thank heavens Gladys Heldman was difficult. It meant she stood up for the things she believed in. It meant she wouldn't back down. It means she and the Original 9 players started what has become the most successful women's pro tour in all of sports.

▼
1971, HRC ladies
helping support the
first NSWCCC

No. 1 in state

FIRST USLTA NATIONAL
WOMEN'S 35 AND SENIOR
CLAY COURT TENNIS CHAMPIONSHIP
MARCH 31 – APRIL 3
HOUSTON RACQUET CLUB

EVENTS: 35 S
35 D
40 S
40 D

DEADLINE – MARCH 15

NATIONAL SENIOR WOMEN'S CLAY COURT CHAMPIONSHIPS – NSWCCC

Each year, HRC hosts the National Senior Women's Clay Court Championship (NSWCCC), which has become the largest women's national championship on the United States Tennis Association (USTA) senior tour. In 1970, concurrent with the first Virginia Slims tournament, the Club started the planning to host the inaugural NSWCCC in 1971. Originally, players were in two age divisions, 35s and 40s, but in the ensuing 45 years, the tournament has expanded to include the odd-year age groups 35s through 85s, adding the 90s in 2016.

The more than 200 entrants include the highest ranking players from the United States, Europe, and many other countries. The NSWCCC committee is made up entirely of HRC members who, in addition to running the tournament, plan a week of events celebrating the camaraderie that is senior women's tennis. Offering the largest prize money to winners in all divisions, the tournament is currently celebrated as the most outstanding in the United States, an achievement owed to the commitment and hospitality of the Club's members, staff, management, sponsors, and volunteers.

"Members of the National Senior Women's Tennis Association report that the NSWCCC is the best in the country. We are very proud of our tournament and each year seek to make this the premier event on the senior tour. As a committee member since the inaugural event, Harriett Hulbert has been our tournament referee for more than 25 years. This greatly contributes to the quality of the NSWCCC."

- Sue Bramlette and Cathy Lassetter, NSWCCC Tournament Directors 2005-present

▶ 1971, Ruth Gross and Nancy Neeld playing in the NSWCCC at HRC

HRC HEAD TENNIS PROS

1966-1968 RICHARD NESMITH

- First tennis professional for HRC
- Worked out of the "shack" at HRC – a small hut constructed near the six original tennis courts
- Played for the University of Houston 1963-1965
- Organized court reservations, gave lessons, and strung rackets

1968-1972 JERRY EVERT

- First Head Pro of the HRC
- Won the 45 and Over Singles tournament at River Oaks where he defeated Bob Kamrath in straight sets
- Illinois and Wisconsin State Champ
- Member of the Notre Dame National Championship Team
- Son Jay played tennis at Rice with HRC's very own Ross Persons
- Niece is the famous Chris Evert

1972-1973 OWEN DAVIDSON

- Won 10 Mixed Doubles Grand Slams – eight with Billie Jean King
- Won a calendar year slam in 1967 in Mixed Doubles by winning the Australian Open, French Open, Wimbledon, and U.S. Open
- Won the 1972 Australian Open Doubles with John Newcomb and the 1973 U.S. Open Doubles with Ken Rosewall
- In 1966 reached the Wimbledon Singles semifinals and Doubles finals
- Inducted into the International Tennis Hall of Fame in 2010
- Inducted into the Australian Tennis Hall of Fame in 2011
- One of only three people to hold the position of Director of Tennis at the All England Lawn Tennis and Croquet Club

1973-1975 SAMMY GIAMMALVA

- Attended the University of Texas where he won three consecutive Southwest Conference Singles titles 1956-1958
- Played for the U.S. Davis Cup team – earning a 7-3 record in match play 1956-1958
- Reached four finals at the Cincinnati Masters
- Reached the quarter finals of the 1955 U.S. National Championships
- Head Coach at Rice University and led the Owls to 10 Southwest Conference titles and twice to the NCAA finals 1959-1972
- Inducted into the Texas Tennis Hall of Fame in 1984

"I am so enthusiastic about the Houston Racquet Club, because I believe it is one of the finest tennis clubs in the country and it happens to be located in the city where I want to live…. I believe the job of a good tennis professional is much more than just giving of the overall program and [I intend to] have as much contact with the membership as possible. I will do the best job that I know to please you and hope that you will support me in this new challenge."

- Sammy Giammalva – HRC Head Pro 1973-1975

From his welcome letter to the membership in the August 1973 *Raconteur*

1976-2006 JIMMY PARKER

- Head Pro of the Houston Racquet Club for 30 years
- Former U.S. Junior Davis Cup
- All-American at Rice University
- Winner of 124 USTA National Championships (as of 2015 tied for the second all-time record)
- Winner of 25 International Tennis Federation World Championships (as of 2015 holds the U.S. record)
- Represented the U.S. on more than 25 World Cup teams (U.S. record)
- Coached hundreds of nationally ranked players of all ages
- Achieved a No. 1 U.S. national ranking in every age group from 35s to 70s and over
- Head Coach of the Rice University tennis team
- Lost to Ken Rosewall on Center Court at the inaugural U.S. Open at Forest Hills in 1968, becoming "the First Loser of the Open Era"
- 1983 United States Professional Tennis Association Player of the Year (1982 Texas Player of the Year)
- Inducted into St. Louis Tennis Hall of Fame, Missouri Valley Tennis Hall of Fame, Rice Athletic Hall of Fame, and Texas Tennis Hall of Fame

2006-PRESENT THOMAS COOK

- Texas Tech team captain and No. 1 Singles and No. 1 Doubles player
- 1989 winner of the Art Foust Sportsmanship Award
- 1990 Southwest Conference Doubles Champion
- 1992 No. 1 ranked Men's Doubles and Mixed Doubles player in Texas
- Played the International Tennis Federation pro satellite circuit
- Joined HRC as Tennis Pro in 1996, promoted to Head Pro in 2006

"My parents were members of HRC when I was a little kid. I took lessons from Jimmy Parker when I was eight. I played other sports a bit growing up, baseball and basketball, but by 12 I concentrated solely on tennis… Dad always asks about my $40,000 backhand."

-Thomas Cook – Head Pro at HRC

CLIFF TYREE – HRC TENNIS PRO 1972-2012

For 40 years, Cliff Tyree was a favorite HRC tennis pro. In February 2012, he passed away after a long illness but left a legacy as an outstanding man and friend to many. In his *Houston Chronicle* obituary from February 10, 2012, his family recounted that he used to say, "He never had to work a day in his life." He was a beloved tennis teacher and left his mark at the Club and in the lives of thousands of members whom he coached over the years.

In March 1985, the *Raconteur* began publishing a column titled "Cliff Notes." Members looked forward to seeing the often strange, but always interesting tidbits Cliff came up with in each issue. For more than 25 years, members marveled at how Cliff could find such humorous, perplexing statistics and information. He also entertained Club members on weekends with his The Really Brothers Band – a mix of country, folk and jazz.

To honor Cliff's memory, the Club established the Cliff Tyree Beautification Project, which helped fund the replacement of over 200 trees that were lost around the Club in the drought of 2011 as well as to enhance the landscaping at the Club. A permanent brass plaque now sits near the pro shop honoring his life and the hundreds of members who gave in support of the project.

HRC TENNIS LEGEND

"I think maybe my friend Cliff would be a bit embarrassed to be called a true gentleman. But I will call him that anyway. If being kind, good natured, sincere, unpretentious, courteous, consistent, dependable, slow to anger, unassuming, respectful, humble, and a myriad of other fine qualities, are the marks of a true gentleman, then certainly he was one."

- Jimmy Parker – Head HRC Tennis Pro 1976-2006

"Cliff Tyree was running a group session for some juniors. They were particularly unruly so Cliff pointed at the court sign on the fence and hit a ball right at it…hit the sign smack in the middle. He told the kids that the next one that's not paying attention would get one in the back of the head. He had no further problems with that group for the rest of the summer."

- Ross Persons – HRC Tennis Pro 1992-Present

◄
Early 1980s, Tennis Pro Cliff Tyree with his young players

Facts and Figures That May Help Your Game

by Cliff Tyree

1. There are two types of people in the world. Those that take their warm up tops off first and those that take their warm up bottoms off first. Look around you.
2. President James Garfield could write Latin with one and hand and Greek with the other simultaneously! Leonardo de Vinci could draw with one hand and write with the other, also simultaneously.
3. Most points are lost not won. Ask Dr. Allen Kline. On Dec. 10, 1985, Dr. Kline beat Ray Newman 6-4 and won only 3 points.
4. A Hard Boiled Egg will spin, an uncooked or Soft Boiled Egg will not.
5. The first people to play on our new lighted court -1 were Marvin Myers and John Freeman. They were asked never to play there again.
6. There are 9 positions in Baseball, 11 in Football, 5 in Basketball, and only 2 in Tennis. In Tennis, they are the Baseline and the Net . . .
7. The Pro Staff went for a group Brain Scan. They were charged 5,000 dollars for a finder's fee.
8. The tension of your strings may be more important than the type of Racquet you use.
9. Connie Francis has sold more records than any female recording artist in history.
10. The cheaper the grapes are the sweeter the taste of the wine.

Happy New Year

Cliff

Amazing Facts and Figures That May Help Your Game

by Cliff Tyree

No, this is not the hottest summer of all time.

1. On July 1, 1987, Doris Bernard and Barbara Hurwitz played tennis for the first time in a year. They could only play for 30 minutes because Doris had to go home and fix supper. Ease up Larry!
2. Bo Jackson was not the first Heisman Trophy winner to play major league baseball. Vic Janowicz won the Heisman Trophy and played baseball for the Pittsburgh Pirates.
3. Superman flunked his physical during World War II, when he read the eye chart in the next room by mistake.
4. There are some things the players we watch on T.V. do that we can't do. . . the one thing they do that makes them so good we can do . . . get our racket ready.
5. While participating in a clinic at the HRC a few years ago, Jose Gross introduced himself to George Adams. They had attended school together in Cuba when they were 6 years old, a few years ago.
6. The left hand performs 56% of typing.
7. Remember you are a tennis player first and a line caller second, and it is not illegal to return a ball and then call it out.
8. An owl, specifically, the great horned owl, is the only animal that will eat a skunk. The wise old owl?
9. During this hot weather, try to take breaks every time you change sides, don't wait until you get tired to start taking breaks, it's too late!
10. I am amazed at how people break our speed limit of 55 and sometimes 60 mph, especially in 30 and 35 mph speed zones.

From various *Raconteurs* with highlighted *"Cliff Notes."*

FACTS AND FIGURES THAT MAY IMPROVE YOUR GAME

by Cliff Tyree

1. Bob Cornforth and Jane Firbank never lost a set in the Lunch Bunch.
2. Miloslav Mecir is the #27 ranked player in the World.
3. The number of hours one practices does not necessarily determine the Rate of Improvement.
4. Remember it is difficult to hit low and deep. It is easier to hit high and deep.
5. Castor Oil is used as a lubricant in jet planes.
6. While 7 men in 100 have some form of color blindness, only 1 woman in 1,000 suffers from it.
7. It is not against the rules to use your brain when you play.
8. Water is the best liquid to drink on hot days.
9. Camels hair brushes are not made of camels hair. They were invented by a man named Mr. Camel.
10. Jim Timmons had the only correct answer to last month's trivia question. He correctly named Chuck McKinley & Frank Froehling of Trinity in 1962 as the only college team to have the number 1 & 2 players in the nation. Jim Parker and Cliff Tyree knew this well playing for Rice and U & H at the same year. Sometimes when they played Trinity, they would play Froehling at Number 1 so you got a big break and only had to play the Number 2 player in the nation.

1973, Linda Perlman taking a lesson from Betty Washington, one of the first women to teach at HRC

1992-PRESENT ROSS PERSONS

- No. 1 Singles and No. 1 Doubles player at Rice University
- Winner of 14 medals (three Gold, five Silver, and six Bronze) in the International Tennis Federation's World Senior Championships and holds 11 United States National Championships in Singles, Doubles, and Mixed Doubles
- World ranking highs: No. 1 Men's 55 Doubles, No. 2 Mixed 55 Doubles, and No. 4 Men's 50 Singles
- Ranked No. 1 in Texas in Men's Open Singles and Doubles, and Mixed Doubles
- Ranked No. 1 in the U.S. Senior Divisions and ranked in the top five more than 10 times

1993-PRESENT RANDY DRUZ

- Played four years at Indiana University, team captain the last two years
- Illinois State High School Champion – Doubles and Team titles
- Played in most major pro tournaments in the world (Wimbledon, U.S. Open, Australian Open, French Open, Tournament of Champions, etc.)
- Played five years on the Association of Tennis Professionals (ATP) Tour, coached by HRC Head Tennis Pro Jimmy Parker
- Achieved an ATP ranking as high as 180 in the world (out of 1300)
- Member of both the ATP and United States Professional Tennis Association with Professional One Certification

HRC AND THE
HOUSTON TENNIS ASSOCIATION

When HRC was established, the bylaws provided that $2 per member per month would be given to the Houston Tennis Association (HTA). The Club bylaws also allowed for the elimination of the $2 fee if desired. In September 1971, a Club vote was taken and the response to the proposal for discontinuing the charge was overwhelming – 603 voted against the fee, 95 voted in favor of it, and at the October annual meeting that year, the Club officially did away with the HTA fee. However, HRC has remained a big supporter of the HTA. Many HRC members have been leaders of the HTA as Presidents and Board members, and the Club has hosted and sponsored many tournaments over the years.

HTA Past Presidents who were also HRC members: James Walsh, Louis Fisher, George Mitchell, Karl Kamrath, Robert Kurtz, Tom McCleary, Jack Blanton, Robert Kamrath, Robert "Rennie" Baker, William Black, Tom Gillis, Towson Ellis, Richard Schuette, Leona Schroeder, Bob Marco, Harriett Hulbert, and Emily Schuette Schaefer

"The HTA is extremely grateful for the Houston Racquet Club's long-standing hospitality for our organization. The Club's donation of court time for our tournaments has enhanced our events and pleased the many players who competed at one of Houston's finest tennis facilities."
- Harriett Hulbert – HRC member, HTA Past President, Texas Tennis Hall of Fame member,
HTA Executive Director Emeritus

1971, LtoR, Monta Mae Mejlaender, Leslie Creekmore and Bambi Schuette getting ready for the Virginia Slims Invitational

2008 HRC WINS "ORGANIZATION OF THE YEAR" FROM THE USTA

In 2008, HRC was named the "Organization of the Year" by the United States Tennis Association (USTA). The award is given to the organization that best exemplifies service to the community, service to its members through junior and adult programs, and service to the game of tennis. According to the USTA, this award represents the standard that all USTA member organizations strive to achieve. In order to win the national award, HRC won the 2007 USTA Texas Sectional "Organization of the Year," which in turn allowed the Club to be nominated for the overall United States award.

March 2008

HOUSTON RACQUET CLUB

RACONTEUR

HOUSTON RACQUET CLUB
WINNER OF THE

USTA
TM

ORGANIZATION OF THE YEAR
AWARD FOR THE ENTIRE

Early-1990s, Jack Deaver and Joan McCleary - getting a laugh out of being Queen of the Hill

HRC KING OF THE HILL

Ever wonder how and when it was started? Bob McFarland, HRC President 1983-1984, had played on a King of the Hill court while he lived in New Jersey, and in 1984 he decided to give it a try here. Fellow member Sherman Hink volunteered to make a sign with the rack for the tennis racquets so people could get in line to challenge the winners. Court 1 became the most popular court on weekend afternoons!

1970, HRC Head Pro Jerry Evert offering tennis lessons to girls in bikinis

1971, LtoR, Betty Pratt, Peggy Landtroop, Evelyn Houseman, and Louise Clapp after playing in the National Senior Women's Clay Court Championships at HRC

THE WORLD OILMAN'S
TENNIS TOURNAMENT – THE WOTT

In 1977, HRC hosted the first World Oilman's Tennis Tournament (WOTT) – now the largest and most important tennis event in the world of energy. The event was founded with the specific goal in mind to provide a way for senior management, energy company owners, and CEOs to socialize and network in a casual and informal way. The invitation only event would meet once a year, closely coinciding with Houston's annual Offshore Technology Conference, and it now attracts a Who's Who of energy business leaders. In 1993, the WOTT became a non-profit organization that annually supports over a dozen charities, mainly those with a focus on children and tennis such as Special Olympics, National Junior Tennis League, and the Richards Foundation.

The first WOTT Chairman was W. Dale Culwell – who, perhaps coincidentally was also on the HRC Board of Directors at the time – and the Tournament Director was Bill Sherman. The tournament format is to hold three days of men's doubles and mixed doubles. WOTT players include all levels of tennis acumen – tennis ability is not a criteria for participation. Although prizes are awarded to players during the event, winning is not the goal; it's a social occasion. The tournament always has several evening events that include dinner and dancing.

The first tournament roster included 341 people with a waiting list. That waiting list has remained almost every year, and an invitation to play is coveted by those in the energy industry. Many current members of the WOTT are considered legacy tournament players since they are second generation, and now the tournament has even a few third generation players.

Many of the biggest energy and service companies are sponsors of the event.

The WOTT has a few annual traditions such as strawberries and vanilla ice cream, and peanut butter and honey on saltines. And although the WOTT has never been rained out, the weather hasn't been perfect some years.

The event founders determined that HRC was the only facility in Houston that could reasonably accommodate the WOTT with the Club's ample courts and dining facilities. The WOTT has gifted the Club many things over the years, including benches, trees, and the "Moment in Time" statue.

▼
1977, Original
WOTT program

▶
2013, WOTT at HRC

WORLD OILMAN'S
TENNIS TOURNAMENT, INC.

WÖTT

BOARD OF DIRECTORS

Wayne Adams
McCormick Oil & Gas

Richard Barnett
Tenneco Oil Co.
Lafayette

Louis Brandt
The Brandt Co.

Dallas Cantwell
Chemical Enterprises

John W. Cooke, Jr.
Barber Oil

Harry Cullen
Quintana Petroleum

John Davis
Reed Tool

Mike Fadden
Houston Oil & Minerals

Jim Fambrough
Union Texas Petroleum
Lafayette

Ed Farrell
Patterson Services, Inc.

Fred Govreau
Union of California

Tom Hart
Shell

John Hill
Exxon Co. U.S.A.

Bill Howell
Wm. F. Howell & Associates

Chuck Jenness
Mid American Oil & Gas

Dan Johnson
Tenneco

John Lollar
Pen Oreille

Bill Low
Oxy Petroleum, Inc.

Elliott McConnell
General Crude

Wayne Miller
Miller Energy, Inc.

Ralph Murphy
The Western Co.

Tom Oliphint
Schlumberger

Harry Pringle
Pringle Petroleum

John Read
Read Energy

Mike Rutherford
Rutherford Oil

Ron Townsend
NL Atlas Bradford

Ken Wax
Grant Oil Country Tubular

Peter White

"In the early days, there were several occasions where partygoers ended up in the pool at some time during the evening. Boys will be boys, right? They decided to end the practice due to safety concerns."

- Jimmy Parker – HRC Head Tennis Pro 1976-2006

"WOTT held a tennis exhibition match as entertainment. We'd arrange for a couple of pros to play matches on Court 1…in the old configuration. One year, to spice up the game, we dressed a chimp in tennis clothes and gave him a racquet. In the first game, the chimp's human partner missed a volley. The chimp hit the guy on the head with the racquet, ran into the woods, and climbed a tree. It took three hours to get him back."

- John Talbot – WOTT Board member and HRC member

CHAPTER FOUR
TENNIS TITANS

HE KNEW THAT IF HIS DREAM TO BUILD A
FIRST-CLASS TENNIS CLUB IN HOUSTON WAS
GOING TO COME TO FRUITION, HE NEEDED
TO ATTRACT THE CITY'S TOP PLAYERS.

THERE IS LITTLE DOUBT THAT GEORGE MITCHELL WAS A VISIONARY. BUT HE WAS ALSO A REALIST. AND HE KNEW THAT IF HIS DREAM TO BUILD A FIRST-CLASS TENNIS CLUB IN HOUSTON WAS GOING TO COME TO FRUITION, HE NEEDED TO ATTRACT THE CITY'S TOP PLAYERS.

That's exactly what he did.

But what is extraordinary is that he didn't just bring in a handful of Houston's best. He brought in the best of the era, all of whom wanted to be part of a club that was the envy of the tennis world. And during its 50-year history, HRC has continued to attract and produce hundreds of players and teaching pros who have been at the pinnacle of their game. HRC for many decades has had more players ranked statewide and nationally than any other club in Texas.

What is especially noteworthy is the fact that many Club members and pros not only played at the top level as children and young adults, but also continued to compete later in life. Some have even played on the international stage (or courts) into their 80s and 90s.

Make no mistake: Most members of HRC are "regular" social players. But the Club's history is also highlighted by a long list of members and pros who have gone on to achieve tennis greatness and honors at many levels – international tournaments, national and state rankings, halls of fame from various schools and states, college championships, and All-American recognition.

HRC and its members are proud to be associated with so many remarkable players and pros. Here is the Club's own unique Roster of Greatness.

◄

1968, LtoR, Nancy Neeld and
Betty Pratt encourage Scott
Mueller who was helping as a
tournament ball boy

HOUSTON RACQUET CLUB
MEMBER AND PRO
TENNIS SUPERSTARS

INTERNATIONAL TENNIS HALL OF FAME MEMBERS

CRITERIA: Induction into the International Tennis Hall of Fame is the highest honor in the sport of tennis. Induction acknowledges an individual's excellence in on court achievements and contributions to the growth of the sport.

OWEN DAVIDSON
GLADYS HELDMAN

GRAND SLAM CHAMPIONS

CRITERIA: Grand Slam Winner – Australian, French, Wimbledon and United States

BRUCE BARNES – Bruce was one of America's greatest tennis players. He was the first ever to win both singles and doubles titles of the Southwest Conference each of his three years of varsity competition (1929, 1930, 1931). The only other player to ever achieve that since is Sammy Giammalva Sr. – an HRC Tennis Pro. In three years of college tennis, Bruce never lost a match. In 1931, he teamed with fellow HRC member Karl Kamrath to win the National Collegiate Doubles title. Barnes played professional tennis from 1932-1943 on the U.S. Pro Championship circuit. He was part of the original HRC charter group to join the Club in 1965 and remained a member for 25 years. He was inducted into the Texas Tennis Hall of Fame in 1981 and passed away in 1990.

OWEN DAVIDSON – Known as "Davo," Owen was one of the world's greatest doubles players. A champion of 11 major mixed doubles titles (eight with Billie Jean King), he is one of just 13 players in history who have won a calendar year Grand Slam in mixed doubles. He won five doubles majors at Wimbledon and the U.S. Championships (which later became the U.S. Open). His four Wimbledon victories are the most mixed doubles crowns at the All England Club for a male player. From 1967 to 1974, the pairing of Billie Jean and Owen produced flawless doubles play. Owen was 6-foot-1 and presented a huge obstacle at net; with Billie Jean's speed and reflexes, the duo produced a game that was unmatched. Owen was the HRC Head Tennis Pro from 1972-1973. He left the Club to return to the professional tour full-time.

RICHEY RENEBERG – In 1974, Richey began playing tennis at HRC when he was nine. From age 10 to 18, he was ranked No. 1 in his age category in Texas. At Southern Methodist University, he was an All-American three times and ranked the No. 1 collegiate player in the country. In 1987, he began his professional career. He reached No. 20 in the world in singles in 1991 and 1996. In 1992, he won the U.S. Open in doubles and went to the finals at Wimbledon. He was also ranked No. 1 in doubles in 1993. He won the Australian Open in doubles in 1995 and played on the U.S. Davis Cup team five times and in the Atlanta Olympic Games in 1996. You can still find him playing on the courts at HRC, often in doubles exhibitions, which are held several times a year.

GRAND SLAM MAIN DRAW PLAYERS

MEMBERS OF THE GRAND SLAM FINAL EIGHT CLUB

CRITERIA: Reached the Final Eight of a Grand Slam – Australian, French, Wimbledon and United States

Bruce Barnes

Owen Davidson

Ron Fisher

Sammy Giammalva Jr.

Sammy Giammalva Sr.

Julie Heldman

Tommy Ho

Richey Reneberg

CRITERIA: Played in the Main Draw of a Grand Slam – Australian Open, French Open, Wimbledon or U.S. Open

Richard Barker

William Barker

Bruce Barnes

John Been

Chris Bovett

Jack Brasington

Owen Davidson

Randy Druz

Ted Erck

Ron Fisher

Sammy Giammalva Jr.

Sammy Giammalva Sr.

Tony Giammalva

Zan Guerry

Ann Heim

Gladys Heldman

Julie Heldman

Julius Heldman

Tommy Ho

Jack Jackson

Daryl Gralka Lerner

Mark Meyers

Graydon Oliver

Jim Parker

Richey Reneberg

Lamar Roemer

Michael Russell

Richard Schuette

Peter Svensson

Jim Ward

"Tennis has been amazing to me throughout my life. I have been playing since I was six and aspire to play until 96! Some of my very best friendships and memories have been made through tennis, and I look forward to many more."

- Matthew Bain

Sue Bramlette

"When I married Bob in 1981, he suggested I take a tennis lesson. I had played soccer, basketball, and volleyball at Vanderbilt – pre Title IX. So in 1982 I took my first lesson at HRC from Jane Firbank Hernandez. Shortly thereafter I began taking weekly lessons from Jim Parker. That relationship resulted in my first national championship five years later (followed by several more), 20 years of teaching at HRC, and a full tennis scholarship for my daughter, Christie, to the University of Virginia. Thank you once again to Jim and all of the pros at HRC!!!!"

-Sue Bramlette

NATIONAL JUNIOR CHAMPIONS

CRITERIA: Winner of a Grand Slam Junior Championship,
Winner of a National Junior Hard or Clay Court, Spring or Winter Championship

Allan Boss

Harry Fowler

Sammy Giammalva Jr.

Sammy Giammalva Sr.

Tony Giammalva

Zan Guerry

Julie Heldman

Julius Heldman

Steve Herzog

Tommy Ho

Ann Hulbert Hopper

Jack Jackson

Karl Kamrath Sr.

Jim Parker

Richey Reneberg

Michael Riechmann

Jennifer Embry Russell

Michael Russell

Richard Schuette

USTA SECTION, DISTRICT OR COLLEGIATE TENNIS HALL OF FAME

CRITERIA: Members of a USTA Section, District (State)
or Collegiate Tennis Hall of Fame

Bruce Barnes

John Been

Kappie Clark Boles

Chris Bovett

President George H. W. Bush

Towson Ellis

John Embree

Ron Fisher

Sammy Giammalva Jr.

Sammy Giammalva Sr.

Jeannie Sampson Kamrath Gonzales

Zan Guerry

Gladys Heldman

Julie Heldman

Harriett Hulbert

Bob Kamrath

Karl Kamrath Jr.

Karl Kamrath Sr.

Meyers Family – Meg Smith, Mark Meyers

George Mitchell

Jim Parker

Richey Reneberg

Richard Schuette

Travis Smith

"My first memories of HRC are from the 1970s, watching the best players of the era playing with their small head wood rackets and white clothing in front of the HRC pro shop on the clay courts. Players such as Harold Solomon, Sherwood Stewart, Zan Guerry, and Jim Parker would play three-hour matches and do battle. To win a point, a player would have to grind out and work to gain an advantage and increase the advantage with each stroke or work to get back into a point with each forehand or backhand. Each shot seemingly had a purpose. Outright winners were a rarity. The fire, concentration, and collegial competitiveness of these players were quite evident. While the game has changed dramatically and is quite different today, their style of play, competitiveness, and never quit attitude have certainly been very influential to my tennis game and approach to life."

- Mickey Branisa

"Tennis for a lifetime. Turning 70 was a significant birthday. To prove that there were still challenges to meet, my daughter, Emily Schaefer, and I competed in all four Super Senior National tournaments and won a Golden Grand Slam. We were honored at the USTA meeting in New York. Fun.

"My husband, Richard Schuette, grew up close to the old municipal courts (now Fonde Center on Sabine Street) living with his grandparents. The tennis pro there acted as his substitute father, giving him a job selling drinks at the tennis center and encouraging his tennis. When time came for college, he attended the University of St. Thomas on an academic scholarship and rolled and painted lines on the clay courts at the new Memorial Park Tennis Center. Next was time for UTMB Medical School when a group of older players pitched in to pay for his first year in medical school. Tennis was a big factor in his growing up. He continued to play and was ranked No. 1 in Men's 35D and Men's 45D, playing with his longtime friend John Been. Tennis was very significant in his life.

"I met Richard when I was about 12 and my mother made me take tennis lessons. We were married for 43 years. We won lots of husband-and-wife tournaments at HRC and other places."

- Bambi Schuette

OUTSTANDING COLLEGE PLAYERS

CRITERIA: NCAA National or Conference Championship Winner or Intercollegiate Tennis Association (ITA) All-American

Richard Barker

William Barker

Bruce Barnes

John Been

Jack Brasington

Ron Fisher

Sammy Giammalva Sr.

Tony Giammalva

Zan Guerry

Ann Heim

Ann Hulbert Hopper

Karl Kamrath Sr.

Richard Keeton

Ron Latta

Michael McSpadden

Mark Meyers

Tammy Christensen Morris

Graydon Oliver

Jim Parker

Adam Putterman

Richey Reneberg

ITF WORLD SENIOR CHAMPIONS

CRITERIA: Winner of an International Tennis Federation Championship; ranked No. 1 in the World by the International Tennis Federation

Jim Parker

Ross Persons

"My fondest memories of growing up were at HRC.

"My mom, Harriett Hulbert, caught the tennis bug in the late 1960s early 1970s. She would put me in daycare twice a day so she could have two tennis games. Finally, when I was eight years old, she put me in a tennis clinic (while she was playing) and I loved it from the beginning. All the kids learned tennis from Betty Washington on Court 2, which is where the swimming pool and diving boards are now!

"I would have to say my greatest memories were playing almost every day with Tammy Christensen Morris when we were in high school. We didn't go to school for very long and would meet daily at two p.m. to play a couple of sets and run some line races together. We made each other better and loved hanging together.

"In the summer of 1984, I had just returned from losing a tight match in the NCAA semifinals, and Cliff Tyree walked by me while I was practicing on Court 20 and just said, 'Great tourney.' It made my day and summer to know 'old' friends were at HRC pulling for me."

- Ann Hulbert Hopper

"I loved playing Father & Son tournaments with Dad. We were No. 1 in Texas for several consecutive years. My most memorable match was losing to the great Bobby Riggs and his son Larry in the National Father & Son Championships the only time it was held at HRC. Mr. Riggs had us beaten before we left the locker room with his gamesmanship and banter!"

-Mitch Creekmore

Mitch Creekmore

"I spent most of my childhood growing up running the grounds of HRC and playing tennis. The things I remember most are the Snack Shack and pecan balls. I remember the grill manager, Ellie, who ran that grill with an iron fist. I remember playing tennis all day and night with a group of kids that are now mostly members as adults. I remember Richard Schuette yelling all the time on the court with John Been. I loved Dr. Schuette. Last but not least was the pro shop that housed most of the tennis junkie kids. The pro shop had a great staff that taught us so much about life. I am so glad that I have the opportunity to be a member as an adult and raise my kids at the Club."

-Tammy Morris

▲
Tammy Morris

NATIONAL SENIOR AND SPECIAL EVENT CHAMPIONS

CRITERIA: Winner of a USTA National Senior Hard, Clay, Indoor or Grass Championship, Winner of a USTA National Father & Son, or Mother & Daughter Championship

Lovie Beard

John Been

Bill Bonham

Sue Bramlette

Rob Collins

Tony Dawson

Towson Ellis

Heidi Gerger

Ria Gerger

Sammy Giammalva Jr.

Sammy Giammalva Sr.

Zan Guerry

Julius Heldman

Kristin Hess

Helen Johnson

Karl Kamrath Sr.

Mark Meyers

Chris Parker

Jim Parker

Ward Parker

Ross Persons

Christie Bramlette Pettit

Richey Reneberg

Emily Schuette Schaefer

Bambi Schuette

Richard Schuette

Jennifer Brennan Toney

Betty Gray Washington

MEMBER USA TEAM — ITF WORLD SENIOR TEAM CHAMPIONSHIPS

CRITERIA: Selected by the USTA to represent the United States in the ITF World Senior Team Championships

Bill Bonham

Sue Bramlette

Rob Collins

Tony Dawson

Ron Fisher

Mark Meyers

Jim Parker

Ross Persons

"The Houston Racquet Club has been more than a beautiful Clubhouse surrounded by tall pine trees in a beautiful neighborhood. It has been where I have met some of my longest and best friends as a junior tennis player, trained as a tennis professional, met my wife, and now raise my family. It is a place where my son is now getting his start as a tennis player and life experiences amongst members and staff whom we regard as family. The Houston Racquet Club is my extended family and a place I call home."

-Ted Erck

"I remember how fun my first clinics were with Jerry Evert. We had obstacle courses and lots of targets. I was eight.

"I also remember my first lesson with Sammy Giammalva. After we hit for 10 minutes or so, he called me up to net and said, 'Tennis isn't for people with good posture... You need to crouch and bend your knees.' I was 13.

"Great memories."

-Leland Putterman

Leland Putterman

USTA SECTIONAL CHAMPIONS AND TOP 10 IN THE UNITED STATES

CRITERIA: USTA Section Winner or ranked No. 1 State High School Champion
USTA Top 10 National Men's or Women's Ranking
USTA Top 10 National Junior Ranking
USTA Top 10 National Senior Ranking
USTA Top 10 National Father & Son, Mother & Daughter Ranking

Ed Austin	Towson Ellis	Dot Hines	Bill Richter
Matt Bain	Ted Erck	Tommy Ho	Lamar Roemer
Renee Baker	Jay Evert	Ann Hulbert Hopper	Andrew Roth
Bruce Barnes	Jerry Evert	Jack Jackson	Jennifer Embry Russell
Lovie Beard	Richard Finger	Helen Johnson	Michael Russell
John Been	Bill Fisher	Jerry Joyce	Johnny Rutherford
Jack Blanton	Louis Fisher	Bob Kamrath	Emily Schuette Schaefer
Kappie Clark Boles	Ron Fisher	Karl Kamrath Sr.	Bambi Schuette
Bill Bonham	Harry Fowler	Polly Knowlton	Richard Schuette
Chris Bovett	Mary Kay Gaedcke	Daryl Gralka Lerner	Travis Smith
Norma Boyle	Heidi Gerger	June Levy	Brian Startzman
Sharon Boyle	Ria Gerger	Libby Marks	Howard Startzman
Sue Bramlette	Mary Jo Giammalva	Dale McCleary	Peggy Startzman
Mickey Branisa	Sammy Giammalva Jr.	Joan McCleary	Joe Stephens
John Burrmann	Sammy Giammalva Sr.	Tom McCleary	Melba Stewart
David Coats	Tony Giammalva	Mark Meyers	Jane Strnadel
Rob Collins	Xavier Gonzalez	Mark Mitchell	Alexander Thirouin
Thomas Cook	Fred Gradin	Lamar Morris	Jean Thirouin
Dan Courson	Kalen Gralka	Graydon Oliver	Don Tomasco
Audrey Cox	Zan Guerry	Lawton Park	Jennifer Brennan Toney
Denise Creekmore	Ann Heim	Chris Parker	Betty Gray Washington
Leslie Creekmore	Carrie Heldman	Jim Parker	Graham Whaling
Mitch Creekmore	Gladys Heldman	Bess Persons	Tig Whitfill
Tom Creekmore	Julie Heldman	Ross Persons	Alex Witt
Katie Davis	Julius Heldman	Christie Bramlette Pettit	Diana Zody
Tony Dawson	Davis Henley	Leland Putterman	
Randy Druz	Rafael Herrera	Richey Reneberg	
Ann Ellis	Bruce Herzog	Grant Riechmann	
	Steve Herzog	Michael Riechmann	
	Kristin Hess	Barry Richards	

CHAPTER FIVE

EMPLOYEES – THE KEY TO A SUCCESSFUL CLUB

Late 1970s, Dennis Buslaya, Issac Valdez, Ramiro "Steve" Benevadis, Jose Louis Henriquez and Sergio Barreto, late 1970s

A BEAUTIFUL BUILDING AND LOVELY GROUNDS ARE NOT ENOUGH TO MAKE MEMBERS SHOW UP. IT TAKES A GREAT TEAM.

THE OVERALL SUCCESS OF ANY CLUB IS GENERALLY
A FUNCTION OF THE PEOPLE WHO WORK THERE. A
BEAUTIFUL BUILDING AND LOVELY GROUNDS ARE NOT
ENOUGH TO MAKE MEMBERS SHOW UP. IT TAKES A GREAT
TEAM, AND THE HOUSTON RACQUET CLUB HAS ALWAYS
HAD ONE.

Employees are devoted to the Club – many have worked at HRC for their entire careers, often
more than 30 years. This is unusual in the club world, where most employees stay less than five
years before moving on to the next job. The fact that so many HRC employees have stayed at the
Club for so long says a great deal about the place where they work: Members treat them like family.
They are loved and admired by members.

Employees stay at the same job for a lot of reasons that go beyond good pay and benefits. It's
also important to work for good leaders, and the Club has been fortunate in that regard. HRC
has had only five general managers in its 50-year history; the initial general manager came from
Sagewood Country Club and moved seamlessly into the job at the new HRC. The Club's history is
proof that consistently great leadership translates to a consistently great experience.

Then there's the food. In some ways, food service at a club is no different from food service at
a traditional restaurant. It can't just be good; it has to be better, and earn rave reviews every day.
But there is one major difference: At a club, the chef needs to be aware of the specific needs and
requests of each member. HRC has been fortunate there, too. The fact that the Club has had just
four chefs shows how well each one of them has met – and then exceeded – members' expectations.

In the end, any successful club keeps its members content. As General Manager/COO
Thomas Preuml, CCM says, "Members speak with their feet. And when the Club is busy, it means
members are happy."

HRC GENERAL MANAGERS

DEAN WIEDOWER

- Started at Sagewood Country Club in 1956 and then, after the merger, joined HRC in 1966 as General Manager
- Before Sagewood, served in the Air Force and worked at the Officers' Club at Ellington Air Force Base for two years
- Briefly worked for nine months at the Houston Country Club
- Degree in senior accounting from Colorado College
- Recognized in October 1970 by the Club Managers Association as a Certified Club Manager – a professional equivalent of a Certified Public Accountant – based on education and length of service, a certification that was given only to a small percentage of managers in the country at the time
- Served as President of the Houston Club Managers Association
- Retired from HRC in 1974 after a combined 18 years at HRC/Sagewood
- Father of five children

"Blame part of the good nature of the HRC staff on the club's 6-foot-1 manager – Dean Wiedower. He's characterized as efficient, fair, pleasant, and always calm – quite an accomplishment in a job with such diversity."

- Excerpt from February 1971 *Raconteur*

KURT LECHER

- Hired in 1974
- Left in 1977 to manage a well-known Los Angeles restaurant called Scandia
- Father of two children

"The Club is more than the brick and mortar that hold it together. Instead it's the stories, connections, relationships, and memories the Club environment has promoted."

- Jimmy Parker – HRC Head Tennis Pro 1976-2006

HORST MANHARD

- Born in Munich, Germany, to a family of restaurateurs
- Graduated from the Munich Hotel and Restaurant School
- Worked previously at the Savoy Hotel in London, Hotel Richmond in Geneva, The Hilton in Cairo, and The Royal Hotel in Copenhagen
- Orchestrated a backdoor exit by the Beatles while at the Savoy, avoiding thousands of adoring fans surrounding the hotel
- Moved to the United States in the 1960s and started work at the Warwick Hotel
- Started at HRC in 1977
- Retired in September 2005 after 28 years at HRC
- Father of three children

"At every Board of Directors meeting since 1977, Horst has been at the head of the table seated next to the president, lending his experience and expertise to every committee and project. He is admired and respected by members, directors, and employees alike. Over the past 23 years, Horst has assembled a loyal and professional staff intent on supporting and serving the membership in all areas."

- Nick Nichols – HRC President 1999-2000, from the March 2000 *Raconteur*

STEVEN GRIFFIN

- Hired in October 2005
- Degree from the University of Houston
- General Manager at Greenville Country Club in Wilmington, Delaware, and Clubhouse Manager at the Petroleum Club of Houston before HRC
- Left HRC in 2008 to join the Art Institute of Houston and is now the Academic Director of Culinary Arts
- Father of four children

THOMAS PREUML, CCM

- Hired in September 2008 as HRC's Chief Operating Officer and General Manager
- Born in Austria, earning a culinary degree in 1983
- Moved to Texas in 1984 and worked at a German restaurant on Houston's west side
- Worked 17 years for ClubCorp at clubs in Denver and Houston
- Board member/Le Comité Permanent of Les Amis d'Escoffier Society of Houston
- Earned the distinction from the Club Managers Association of America (CMAA) as a Certified Club Manager
- Established HRC annual holiday tradition of donating the Gingerbread House display and monetary contributions from HRC members to MD Anderson Children's Cancer Hospital
- Married and father of one son

"Thomas is a gifted leader who inspires pride and dedication from his staff. Not only does the membership recognize his ability to manage, but those who work with him on a daily basis have the utmost respect for him. He has instituted employee training, daily wait staff reviews, a consistent comment card process for members, closing reports for each restaurant, and many other efficiencies and improvements that have led to a better managed club."

- Excerpt from a 2011 letter signed by almost every past HRC president in support of his nomination for CMAA Club Manager of the Year

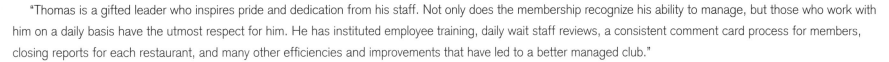

2013, HRC chefs at work in the kitchen

HRC CHEFS

CATALINO LAANAN

- First HRC chef, hired in 1967 at the age of 63
- Born in the Philippines
- Served in World War II and is buried at the Houston National Cemetery
- Retired from HRC in 1973

WINFRIED ULRICH

- HRC Executive Chef 1974-2006
- Born and raised in Heidelberg, Germany
- Trained as a chef's apprentice in Europe for three years
- Moved to Houston in 1965 to work at Hotel America
- Executive Chef at the Flagship Hotel in Galveston and at the Hyatt Regency and Warwick Hotel in Houston
- Retired after 32 years at HRC, bought a ranch in Cuero, Texas, and raises cattle
- Still plays tennis at HRC several days a week

GRANVILLE WOOD

- HRC Executive Chef 2006-2010
- Culinary degree and professional chef certification from George Brown College, Toronto, Canada
- Worked in many restaurants and hotels in Florida and Texas
- Executive Chef at BraeBurn Country Club and The Forest Club in Houston
- Currently the owner and chef at The Blue Goose Café in Fargo, North Dakota

BERNARD HURLEY

- Hired as Executive Chef May 2010
- Born and raised in Chicago
- Graduate of the oldest culinary school in America, the Washburne Culinary Institute
- Worked in many restaurants, hotels, and clubs in the Chicago area
- World-ranked expert chocolatier; trained in Paris with renowned French chefs
- Won second place in 2000 in the U.S. Pastry Competition
- Certified expert coffee taster

LONGTIME HRC EMPLOYEES

35+ YEARS AT HRC

Name	Year		Department
Velma Smith	1974	2010 (Ret.)	Kitchen
James "Cliff" Tyree	1976	2012 (d.)	Tennis Professional
Isaac Valdez	1977		Food & Beverage
Julian Sierra	1979		Courts & Grounds
Ramiro "Steve" Benavides	1980		Security
Adrian "Jorge" Roman	1980		Food & Beverage
Alfredo "Ramon" Garcia	1980		Locker Room

"My responsibility is to keep the mechanical side of the Club working. The wait staff serves the members, but if the lights, AC, ovens, or refrigerators don't work, the whole effort breaks down."

- Raul Osorio – HRC Head of Maintenance, started work at HRC in 1982

"Working at HRC is like working with family. We've all gotten a little older together. It's usually fun to be here. It's really fun to watch the kids grow up.

"One jokester kid found a frog outside one day and put it under a plate at the salad bar. An older lady came to the salad bar and picked up the plate, freeing the frog, who jumped a foot in the air. You can imagine the chaos."

- Carlos Chavez – HRC Grill Manager, started work at HRC in 1983

"I love the little kids. There was one little boy 20 years ago that was always acting up. As a joke, I told him he had to behave or I'd put him in the box, kept in the back room. That usually settled him down. A few years ago, he came back from college, flexed his muscles, and challenged me to 'put him in the box' now."

- George "Jorge" Roman – HRC Waiter, started work at HRC in 1980

1990s, Juan Valencia and Carlos Salazar helping at the annual HRC Middle School Halloween Party

"HRC was known for our flaming desserts. One night, when I was pouring alcohol on a flaming pan, crepes, I think, fire was sucked into the bottle and it exploded. The bottom blew through the room's window and the diner's hair caught fire. Her dress was a mess, spotted with brandy. Fortunately, there was no lasting damage and the members returned for a free meal."

- Winfried Ulrich – HRC Executive Chef 1974-2006

30+ YEARS AT HRC

Dora Cantu	1969	1999 (Ret.)	Ladies Locker Room
Winfried Ulrich	1974	2006 (Ret.)	Executive Chef
Bernard Holloway	1974	2004 (Ret.)	Food & Beverage
Mack Pinkston	1975	2005 (d.)	Kitchen
Jim Parker	1976	2006 (Ret.)	Tennis Professional
Carlos Salazar	1978	2010 (Ret.)	Assistant General Manager
Maria Henriquez	1980	2010 (Ret.)	Janitorial
Antonio Henriquez	1981		Courts & Grounds
Rosa Barreto	1982		Kitchen
Evelyn Bowie	1982		Manicurist/Spa Services
Raul Osorio	1982		Maintenance
Carlos Chavez	1983		Food & Beverage
Cindy Richardson	1983		Swim Instructor

25+ YEARS AT HRC

Horst Manhard	1977	2005 (Ret.)	General Manager
Alejandro Sanchez	1979	2007 (Ret.)	Courts & Grounds
Digna Blanco	1981	2007 (Ret.)	Kitchen
Eduardo "Polo" Alarcon	1987		Locker Room
Juan Valencia	1987	2007 (Ret.)	Food & Beverage
Ubertina "Cristina" Cornejo	1988		Janitorial
Robert "Bob" Triska	1988		Courts & Grounds
Carmen Valencia	1988		Food & Beverage
Marisela Padilla	1989		Locker Room
Jorge Pujol	1989	2014 (d.)	Courts & Grounds
Elmar Delgado	1990	2008 (Ret.)	Food & Beverage
Angel Garcia	1990		Courts & Grounds

◄
1973, Dinner on the
Redwood Terrace

20+ YEARS AT HRC

Name	Year	Retired	Department
Josy Chavez	1985	2005 (Ret.)	Accounting
Ana "Ana Gloria" Hansen	1991		Food & Beverage
Ross Persons	1992		Tennis Professional
Randall "Randy" Druz	1993		Tennis Professional
Lilian "Mabel" Chavez	1993		Food & Beverage
Maria Valle	1993		Kitchen
Rolando Acovera	1994		Food & Beverage
Martha Sierra	1994		Kitchen
Thomas Cook	1996		Tennis Professional
Juana Gomez	1996		Janitorial
Javier Tapia	1996		Food & Beverage

"In the early days at HRC, we used high school kids for valet parking. One year the kids got in a fight and took off. We had all the keys, but no idea where cars were parked. Everyone was involved in trying to find the cars. Never used high school kids again."

"Our first big wedding was in the early 1980s for 1,100 people. After seeing what we could do at the Appreciation Party, a member moved their wedding reception to the Club. We held it on a Monday and they took over the whole Club."

"We have extremely good employee retention at the Club – unusual for clubs in general. Eighty percent of our people are long term. It's become like family… a good place to work."

- Horst Manhard – HRC General Manager 1977-2005

"Sometimes I ride my bike, but usually I walk or run to work. I live about seven or eight miles from the Club near TC Jester and 34th. Most days it takes me about an hour. I leave before four in the morning; sometimes at 3:30. My father always said to get to work a half hour early. The exercise is good for me. My blood pressure and cholesterol are good. I can't do other exercise. This walking is good for me."

- Alfredo "Ramon" Garcia – HRC Locker Room Attendant, started work at HRC in 1980

2013, Chef Bernard Hurley,
center, with Dominic Farino
and Rony Ortiz preparing for
the Escoffier Society Dinner

1980s, Isaac Valdez
displaying a special wine

HRC EXCEPTIONAL EMPLOYEE
EXPERIENCES

HRC employees are required to go through a unique training program called Five Star Service. The program assures HRC members that all employees – new and old – understand the values and culture that make the Club special. It's called Exceptional Experiences, and it empowers employees to continually improve and learn while working at HRC.

The Five Star Service program consists of an orientation followed by five modules of training that covers 13 different service values that are essential to providing an exceptional member experience. The sessions are broken into three different classes for about two hours each. Assistant General Manager Sonny McDaniel is the author of the program and moderator of the classes.

All management staff is also required to go through training for CPR, automated external defibrillator, and First Aid certification. HRC's safety program earned national recognition by the Club Managers Association of America in 2013 by winning first place in the "Safety Programs & Risk Management" category. HRC is considered the gold standard by ClubSafe, a leader in the private club industry for managing safety programs across the country.

Isaac Valdez is a certified sommelier – a distinction only about 160 people in Texas have achieved. In his spare time, he teaches at the Texas Wine School and helps other sommeliers train for their certification.

"Mr. Mitchell arrived at the dining room one night without a tie. I told him that he needed one to stay for dinner. It was the rule back then. He shrugged, went off, and returned with a tie. I don't think he was upset but not many people told Mr. Mitchell anything."

"The most expensive bottle of wine I've sold at the Club was a Chateau La Tour for $1,100. It was a good year, 1956, I think."

- Isaac Valdez – HRC Sommelier, started work at HRC in 1977

GINGERBREAD HOUSE DISPLAY

In 2008, COO/General Manager Thomas Preuml, CCM started what is now an annual holiday tradition at HRC to build an elaborate, large Gingerbread House for display in the lobby. Thomas, Pastry Chef Joy Werner, and Executive Chef Bernard Hurley work for several days building the spectacular exhibition.

The project is part of Thomas' personal history – originally from Austria and a former Executive Chef, he began building an annual Gingerbread House in 1991. Over the years, his creations have ranged from simple log cabins to elaborate reproductions of European castles.

In 1993, the display was donated to MD Anderson Hospital in honor of a family member of Thomas' who was undergoing cancer treatment at the time. In 2009, Thomas began donating the display to the MD Anderson Children's Cancer Hospital along with toys and a monetary donation from the Club and its members. In the past seven years, more than $55,000 has been donated from Club members in support of the project. Several other Houston clubs have joined in the tradition, and in 2014, the Gingerbread House displays filled the hospital lobby for all the cancer patients and their families to enjoy during the Christmas holidays.

2014, Chef Bernard Hurley and COO/General Manager Thomas Preuml, CCM

2013, COO/General Manager Thomas Preuml, CCM working on the HRC Gingerbread House

CHAPTER SIX

THE FUTURE FOR HRC

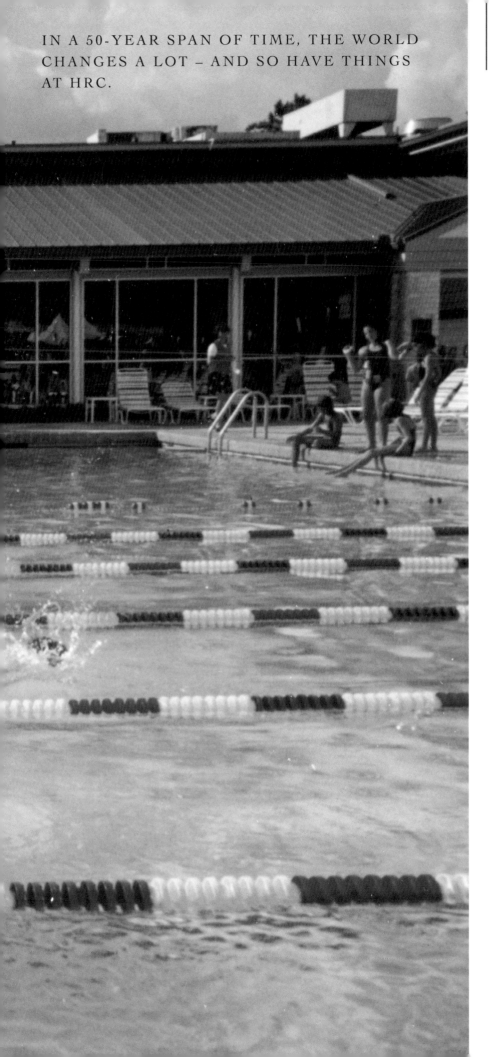

IN A 50-YEAR SPAN OF TIME, THE WORLD
CHANGES A LOT – AND SO HAVE THINGS
AT HRC.

2003, HRC swim
team practice

IN A 50-YEAR SPAN OF TIME, THE WORLD
CHANGES A LOT – AND SO HAVE THINGS
AT HRC. THERE WERE MANY FIRSTS TO
CELEBRATE, NOT ONLY IN THE TENNIS WORLD
BUT IN OTHER AREAS OF THE CLUB AS WELL.
In 1985, HRC voted in its first woman to the board and then 20 years later
elected its first female president. Over time, many changes have taken place
that affected our membership – new categories, honorary members, fees, and
social groups.

And as our membership changed, so did their wants and needs.

Entering the 21st century, the new generation of Club members desired a
world-class fitness center; an Olympic-size heated pool to accommodate the
growing numbers of swimmers; a resort-style pool to respond to the needs of
hundreds of new families with small children; and more social activities to keep
members engaged outside of tennis and dining.

In delivering what the membership asked for, HRC demonstrated once
more that it is an ever-growing, evolving Club. It still is, too. In 2015, members
approved the next big enhancement – a major renovation to the lower level of the
Clubhouse as well as other areas. No doubt founder George Mitchell and original
architect Karl Kamrath would be pleased to see their dream of developing one
of the country's preeminent tennis clubs continuing on a path of success and
achievement.

◄
2004-2005 HRC
President
Fred Saunders,
2005-2006 HRC
President Meg Smith

►
1973, *Raconteur*

THE COST OF MEMBERSHIP

1968: HRC Membership was full at 1,000 with a "sizable" waiting list

1973: Initiation fee increased to $2,500

1977: Initiation fee increased to $4,000

1980: Initiation fee increased to $7,500

1981: Initiation fee increased to $10,000

1986: Initiation fee increased to $12,000

2013: Initiation fee increased to $19,000

2014: Initiation fee increased to $25,000

WOMEN'S FIRSTS

1985-1986 – Sally Tinkham elected the first woman to the HRC Board of Directors.

2005-2006 – Meg Smith elected the first woman HRC President. She was no stranger to "firsts," being in the first female class at the University of Virginia and on the first women's tennis team at LSU.

"At the Grand Opening celebration for the new Fitness Center, resort pools, and Pavilion, we wanted to accomplish several important things. Most importantly, we wanted to honor our rich past and pay homage to the people whose leadership and hard work brought the Club into existence. We invited back to the Club as many past presidents and founding members as we could to see the new, exciting changes."

- Meg Smith – HRC Club President 2005-2006

Spring styles

Spring fashions were featured at the February Women's Association style show by Max's Beauty Show & Boutique. June Levy, president of the WA, introduced the program. Dottie Horlock, above right, modeled, as did Sissy Sparks, below left, and Nancy Sterling, below right.

The three women who put it all together were from left, Fama Blaine, Betty Ellis, Nell Winters.

A CLUB OF MANY MINDS

Over the years, HRC has developed a successful member-driven set of organizations designed to promote business and social networking. These now include:

Women's Association. From almost the Club's beginning, there was a Women's Association. It was formally organized in October 1968 with annual dues of $7.50, which have risen to $35 – an average of less than 60 cents a year, which remains a great deal. The Association sponsors activities that include luncheons, mixers, tennis tournaments, middle school Halloween and Valentine's Day parties, a holiday tea, and the spring style show, and it assists with the National Senior Women's Clay Court Championships.

Along with these activities, the Association also donates major gifts to the Club, sponsors bridge activities, and supports the Gingerbread House project that benefits MD Anderson Children's Cancer Hospital. Additionally, it helps to underwrite the annual HRC Lovie Cup and Roederer Cup Pro-Am tennis tournaments.

Men's Association. Established in 2012, the Men's Association is aimed at promoting friendship and camaraderie among its members; bringing into closer fellowship all men and their families within HRC; and providing support for the various activities, from athletic to social.

HRC Oil and Gas Society. The mission of the Oil and Gas Society is to provide a platform for members working in or with the oil and gas industry to network and socialize among their peers while fostering member relationships. The group meets several times a year with evening receptions and hosts an annual Oil Barons Ball.

HRC Wine Committee and Uncork'd Wine Society. The HRC Wine Committee's mission is to generate first-class wine-related events and tastings as both an opportunity for wine education and a chance to draw both novice and advanced wine lovers together in a forum that enhances their Club experience. Members join the Uncork'd Wine Society, which meets many times a year for wine tastings and dinners.

HRC SENIOR STATUS AND
THE CLUB'S NEW AGE

In October 1985, the Club voted to change the bylaws to establish a Senior Membership category to allow more members to join. Voting Members of a certain age who have spent a certain length of time as Voting Members could go "senior" – no longer Voting Members, with reduced dues – allowing new members to join and still keep the Club within the 1,000-member limit.

As time passed and the membership changed, we saw some shifts in our "demographics," too. In 2008, the average age of a member was 62. In 2015, it was 50 – and the average for a new member was 42. Not only that, but in 2015 we had members join who were as young as 23 and as old as 92!

WHAT DO YOU DO WHEN YOU CAN'T
PLAY TENNIS ANYMORE?
SENIORS SETTING A NATIONAL TREND

In 2012, HRC entered our Senior Pilot Program in the Club Managers Association of America national contest for innovative ideas. The Club won the first-place trophy and blue ribbon for developing the best new program in the country. Our program involves all sorts of activities that appeal to senior members: a book club, exercise program, outside speakers, book reviews, luncheons, dinners, dance lessons, and popular off-site trips to destinations both in Houston and around the state. Our seniors program is now used as a model for other clubs across the country, and stands as a shining example of how to maintain senior involvement and membership retention.

2006, President George H.W. Bush welcoming students during lunch in the Grill

▼

President George H.W. Bush and Barbara arriving for lunch

PRESIDENT BUSH JOINS

1993 – U.S. President George H.W. Bush accepted HRC's invitation to be one of the Club's first Honorary Members.

"Neil Bush must have told his father that I'd been helpful to him. President Bush decided he wanted to meet me and sent his Secret Service people back to the locker room to get me. When four very official guys showed up looking for me, I was frightened. What had I done? Turned out to be one of the greatest moments of my life."

- Alfredo "Ramon" Garcia – HRC Locker Room Attendant, started work at HRC in 1980

"President George H.W. Bush often lunched at the Club. I always looked after him. His secretary called one afternoon to say President Bush wanted to invite me to a movie opening in Houston, 'Up in the Air' with George Clooney. Sent me four tickets. They called twice to make sure I'd be there. When I arrived, I was welcomed as President Bush's friend, not a waiter at HRC. I was honored."

- Carlos Salazar – HRC Assistant Manager 1978–2009

HRC POOL PROGRAM

In the summer of 1969, an HRC swim team was established under the watchful eye of Fred Breckwoldt, who was the varsity swim coach at Rice. HRC's team, called the Manta Rays, joined the Southwest Aquatic League, which included most of our neighboring clubs. The first summer, we had 147 swimmers; the turnout was so large we had to divide into two teams. HRC participated in 10 swim meets that summer, finishing with eight wins and just two losses. The next year, we added a synchronized swim team and a diving team to the program.

In 2015, the Manta Rays remain a strong team with a head coach, 13 assistant coaches, and more than 200 swimmers. No longer just organized for the summer months, HRC's program has more than 30 swimmers who train year-round. Our members checked in at the pool desk more than 8,000 times in 2015. So as you can imagine, the pools stay very busy.

THE GREAT SWIMSUIT SCANDAL

As told by Bob McFarland, HRC President 1983-1984:

"In the early 1970s, the female lifeguards at the pool wore one-piece swimsuits. As fashions changed, the swimsuits began to be cut up higher on the side, and our lifeguards began to adopt the newer fashion. Some of the women members of the Club decided that the girls' swimsuits were too revealing for HRC, and they formed a committee. One day I was sitting on the patio after tennis, and a representative of the committee confronted me about the scandalous attire of our lifeguards. I quickly turned it over to the Pool Committee, and they established a more conservative guideline for the female lifeguards."

▶ 2013, HRC
swim meet:
LtoR,
Emily Hardin,
Lily Sellers,
Belicia Pond

"One of the members, Jack Ort, I think, had played in the heat and came in really dragging. Rather than cooling down, he jumped in the whirlpool and ordered some hot soup from Ramon. He came close to passing out, but crawled out and lay down on the edge of the tub. Ramon showed up with the soup and was flummoxed. He put the soup on the ledge, laid the bill on Jack's chest, and ran off to get some help. Jack's story was that he expected this is the way it would all end, lying nude on the floor next to a bowl of soup and an HRC bill on his chest."

- Jimmy Parker – HRC Head Pro 1976-2006

WHERE HAVE THE TOWELS GONE?

For almost 50 years, the Club has been providing towels for members to use, and for almost 50 years, it has been asking for them back. In 1981, HRC said that 8,400 tennis towels and 1,500 bath towels were missing, and reported a cost of $1,000 a month in towel supplies!

◄
2013 swim meet
at HRC

▲
Mid 1970s,
towels stacked
outside the pro shop

HRC FITNESS CENTER

BLAKE STOVALL

- Director of Fitness 2010-present
- Graduated from Texas A&M in Sports Management
- Worked in the private club and fitness industry for 23 years
- Nationally Accredited Certified Personal Trainer for 23 years
- National Swimming Pool Foundation Certified Pool Operator

HRC COURTS AND GROUNDS MAINTENANCE

BOB TRISKA

- Director of Courts and Grounds 1988-present
- Native Texan from El Campo, Texas
- 1976 Texas A&M graduate in Parks Administration
- Cross-functional expertise in Hard, Hydro Grid and Clay Court maintenance
- Advanced landscape design, horticulture, and agronomy expert

◄

2013, Aerial picture
of the resort pools,
Fitness Center and
Pavilion

►

Fitness Center
in action

HRC FITNESS CENTER
GETS A WORKOUT

In 2011, HRC completed a membership survey that listed fitness as the top preferred Club activity. Today it is the main focus for most members, as the Fitness Center averages over 6,000 visits per month. The 17,175-square-foot facility is currently home to 27 indoor cycling bikes, 35 pieces of cardio-type equipment, a 16-piece full line of Cybex strength machines, Pilates equipment, group exercise rooms, and men's and ladies' locker rooms. The fitness activities are coordinated with the help of 34 exercise instructors who teach 70 classes a month.

"A couple of times some raccoons have gotten into the Clubhouse locker room. I'm the guy they call on to get them out. Kind of a 'raccoon whisperer.' One time there were three of them. I lined them up and they followed me outside. Don't know how it happened."

- Alfredo "Ramon" Garcia – HRC Locker Room Attendant, started work at HRC in 1980

Conceptual View of the Adult Dining Bar/Lounge

THE FUTURE PLANS FOR HRC

Although the Club has undergone many renovations and improvements over the past 50 years, the main Clubhouse was due for a major facelift. Parts of it have remained virtually unchanged for those 50 years – the men's and ladies' locker rooms, the grill kitchen, and the location of the grill dining and bar areas. Members are using and enjoying the Clubhouse at unprecedented levels, and a redesign was needed to increase dining capacity and kitchen efficiency.

In April 2015, the membership approved a project that will total about $8 million to renovate the lower part of the Clubhouse, ballroom, and front exterior. Additional work will also take place in the Fitness Center, and there will be parking lot improvements, an expansion of the Redwood Deck, and tennis court refurbishment. This approval followed more than three years of surveys to determine what members wanted, as well as visits to other clubs, countless Long Range Planning meetings, several member focus groups, and town hall-type meetings. For the first time in the Club's history, an assessment was passed with the overwhelming support of the Voting Members.

Conceptual View of Family Dining

Construction should begin in 2016 once architectural plans are finished, the Hunters Creek city engineers approve the plans, and financing is in place. The Clubhouse will remain open during construction. Food service will move upstairs to the dining room and the ballroom while work is underway in the lower level. Plans are to reopen the new restaurant and bar in 2017.

"The issue of building a new Clubhouse was tested, but a strong majority did not favor it. The condition of the existing building is sound and well worth renovating. Our architect and engineers have verified the adaptability and suitability of the existing Clubhouse for renovation."

- Bradford Patt, MD, HRC President 2014-2015

CHAPTER SEVEN

APPENDIX

◄

1967, *The Net Set* magazine - Ken Burroughs, right, hands the first tennis ball to be used on the new courts of HRC to Earl Ricks. Burroughs was Co-chair of the Building Committee.

APPENDIX

Brick Path Supporters
1967-1968 HRC Board of Directors
2015-2016 HRC Board of Directors
2014-2015 HRC Board of Directors
HRC Past Presidents
Women's Association Presidents
Men's Association Presidents
1965-2015 HRC Tennis Pros
Men's Singles Champions
Men's Doubles Champions
Women's Singles Champions
Women's Doubles Champions

50TH ANNIVERSARY BRICK PATH SUPPORTERS

The Houston Racquet Club thanks the generous members and friends who helped underwrite the anniversary year celebration with the purchase of a brick for our 50th anniversary path.

Lindsay & Grant Amburn	Sandy & Kevin Cofer	Angie & David Habachy
Jackie Anderson	Peggy & Jim Cole	Colleen Hagen
Teri & Ronnie Andrews	The Thomas Cook III Family	Rob & Angie Hancock
Tiffany & Robert Aspinall	Mary Elizabeth & Dick Corbin	Angie & Dan Hardin
Roni & Doug Atnipp	The Creekmore Family	Patty Harris
Catherine & Tyler Austin	Billie & Scot Davis	Elizabeth & Michael Hatfield
Peg & Bill Austin	Kimberly & Austin Davis	Ann & Bill Heim
Debra Baker & Peter Rockrise	The Dawson Family	Tessa & Matt Henderson
Courtney & Rich Barrus	Maria & Geoffroy De Rorthays	Barbara & Ernest Henley
Lovie & Earl Beard	Kathy & Matt Deffebach	Phyllis & Sherman Hink
Harriette Bearden	Jaime & David Dilger	Nicole & Will Hodge
Betsy & Craig Beasley	Kim & Chris Dopp	Christine & Ty Hoffer
Christi & JP Bennett	Nora & Peter Dorflinger	Judy & Jim Holcomb
Kate & Eddie Bialas	Cary Dunham	Ashley & Russ Holmsten
Andy & Susan Billipp	Toni Duperier	Linda & Charles Houssiere
The Billipp Siblings – Sarah, Peter, Annie & Elizabeth	Anne & Brady Edwards	HRC Oil and Gas Society
Kim & Ian Bishop	Linda & Bill Earle	HRC Women's Association
Cindy & Robert Blevins	Tom B. Eaton Jr.	Harriett Hulbert
Kappie & Read Boles	Karen & John Edmonds	Angie & Roger Igo
William D. Bonham	Gayette Eicher	Elin & Tommy Jackson
Mary & Jim Boynton	Dayna & Ted Erck	Melinda & Chris Jackson
Sue & Bob Bramlette	Annette & Knut Eriksen	Rebecca & Lee Jackson
Michele & Friedrich Brenckmann	Molly & Kip Ferguson	Mary & Mike Jawor
Kelly & Richard Brink	Nanette & Jerry Finger	The Jenkins Family
The Barrett S. Brown Family	Jonathan & Karen Finger	Judy & Chris Job
Tonja Brown	Amanda & David Fisher	Anna & Scott Johnson
Sidney Brown	Bill Fisher	Ginny & Jason Keyser
Stephanie & Michael Brunner	Ron Fisher	Maude Rose & Allen Kline
Tami & Keith Budd	Kate & John Fitzgerald	Carrie & Jeff Knowles
The Burroughs Family	David Frantz	Jalna & Bill Kottwitz Sr.
Courtney & Kevin Cadwell	Harriet Freeman	Kathy & Bill Kottwitz Jr.
David Chalmers	Natalya & Javier Gonzalez	Ruth & Bob Landauer
Lori & Ike Claypool	Paula & John Goodpasture	Cathy Lassetter
	SaraNan & James Grubb	Chaille Latham

Rhea & Ron Latta

Barbara Jean Lauratis

Leah & John Leggett

Ann & Chip Letton

Carla & Tony Maarraoui

Kelly & Steven Madden

Nancy & Michael Magilton

Leisha & Jeff Mamera

Ashley & Dominic B. Mandola

Eddie Mattei

Rachel & Toby Mattox

Betty & Alan May

Gundi McCandless

Tracy & Ryan McCleary

Hugh E. McGee Jr.

Heather & Ryan McKenzie

Stacy & Stephen McNair

Cheryl & John Meador

Susan & Mark Meyers

Jennie & Ed Miller

Brooke & Michael Monk

Julianna & Scott Moorad

The E.C. Moore Family

Pamela & Bob Moore

Penelope & David Moore

Tammy & Lamar Morris

Melissa & Bill Moss

Meepsie & Craig Murray

Jane Muse

National Senior Women's Clay Court Championships

National Senior Women's Tennis Association

Linda & Nick Nichols

Doug & Glenda Nicholson

Gretchen & Marvin Odum

Amanda & Christopher Ollison

Cynthia & John Onstott

Julie & Keith Page

Christina & Alexander Papandreou

Susan & Bradford Patt

Jane & Elwin Peacock

Paul Peacock

Kim & Eddie Perdomo

Gaye Platt

Maya & Matt Pomroy

Olivia & Matt Porter

Susanne, Alex & Thomas Preuml

The Pringle Family

Veronica & Marcus Pullicino

Hilary & Tim Purcell

Carolyn & Leland Putterman

Jessica & Clint Rancher

Joe D. Reed

Joan & Clark Reid

Shannon & Mitch Reid

Mindy & Sean Rice

Kim & Don Richards

Veronica & Michael Roa

Denise & Gary Roeder

Rotary Club of Memorial-Spring Branch

Casey & Coleman Rowland

Roberta & David Rude

Lilly & Michael Russell

Karen & Rob Saltiel

EllenAnn & Marc Sands

Gayle & Fred Saunders

Lisa & Brett Schrader

Maggie & Walt Schroeder

The Richard Schuette Family

Sue & Steve Shaper

Cindy & Bob Shealor

Peggy & Bill Shrader

Adelaide & Ted Smith

Juanita & John Smith

Meg & Michael Smith

Sharon & Richard Snowden

Elizabeth & Michael Snyder

Jackie & Bob Stagg

Michael Stavinoha & Colleen Hagen

Nancy & Pete Sterling

Lauri & Gib Surles

Catherine & Chris Swinbank

Kay & Bert Tabor

Pat & John Talbot

Allison Tatem

Andrea & Trent Tellepsen

Lara Marie & Aaron Thielhorn

Lesli & Tip Tippit

Christin & Ugo Tombolini

Ned Torian

Katherine & Andrew Tower

Jeni, Gannon & Bear Turner

Laurie & Paul Tyler

Winfried Ulrich

Laurie & Doug Vander Ploeg

Claudia & Andrew Varady

Amy & Erik Voss

Mindy & Adam Voyles

Amy & Rob Wagner

Rachel, Allison & Curt Wegenhoft

Emily & Danny Weingeist

Karen & Hunter White

Mary & Brad White

Laura & Richard Whiteley

Denise & Brad Williams

Jaymie & John Williams

Mary Ellen & Dick Wilson

Carrie & Ron Woliver

Jessica & Brian Womac

The Woods Family

Vereen & Madison Woodward

World Oilman's Tennis Tournament

Ingrid & Michael Wynne

Katherine & Mark Yzaguirre

Kathy and Tom Zay

Davis Cuppers in Exhibition at HRC

Davis Cup stars Bob Lutz and Stan Smith

On Sunday, March 9, the three day gala opening of the Houston Racquet Club was climaxed by a tennis exhibition featuring Davis Cup stars of the present, past, and the future.

Present day cup stars Stan Smith and Bob Lutz defeated past U.S. Davis Cup star Ham Richardson (he helped to bring the cup back from Australia several years ago) and sure fire future cup prospect Bobby McKinley of Trinity.

Smith played Lutz and Richardson traded strokes with McKinley in singles competition prior to the doubles.

The crowd of several hundred applauded the fine tennis which undoubtedly will be a prelude to a major tennis event to be held at the club in the near future.

Wilson's Jim Schulze and Karl Kamrath, Jr. at the exhibition

Former Rice and University of Houston stars Ronnie Fisher and John Been with Carolyn Been at the open house and exhibition

1969,
The Net Set
magazine

1967-1968 HRC BOARD

Oliver M. Bakke Jr.

William B. Black Jr.

Kenneth R. Burroughs

R.R. Cravens

Thomas D. Creekmore

Louis A. Fisher

Edwin W. Hornberger

Charles H. Kerner

Robert W. Kurtz

James. R. (Bob) Lyne Jr.

C. Addison McElroy

Hugh E. McGee Jr.

George P. Mitchell

Joseph H. Stephens

James A. Walsh

William B. White

2014-2015 HRC BOARD

Mark Bragg

Mitch Creekmore

Gayette Eicher

Andy Johnston – Ex-Officio

Leah Leggett

Dominic Mandola

Mark Meyers

Michael Monk

Brad Patt – President

Paul Peacock

Mindy Rice

Kim Richards

Andrew Tower

Mindy Voyles

Brad White

Karen White

2015-2016 HRC BOARD

Mitch Creekmore

John Edmonds

Gayette Eicher

Leah Leggett

Dominic Mandola

Mark Meyers

Michael Monk – President

Lynn Murphy

Brad Patt – Ex-Officio

Paul Peacock

Hilary Purcell

Mindy Rice

Craig Smyser

Mindy Voyles

Danny Weingeist

Brad White

2009-2010 President
Steven Madden,
2008-2009
President Tim Purcell,
1968-1969 President
George Mitchell, COO/
General Manager
Thomas Preuml, CCM

HRC PAST PRESIDENTS

James A. Walsh • 1966-1967	J. David Frantz • 1991-1992
Hugh E. McGee Jr. • 1967-1968	Clark Reid • 1992-1993
George P. Mitchell • 1968-1969	Joe B. Mattei • 1993-1994
William B. White • 1969-1970	George E. Uthlaut • 1994-1995
William. B. Black Sr. • 1970-1971	Robert W. Bramlette • 1995-1996
Kenneth R. Burroughs • 1971-1972	Bob Stephens • 1996-1997
Jack T. Dulworth • 1972-1973	Clyde G. Buck • 1997-1998
Charles L. Wood • 1973-1974	Peter D. Sterling • 1998-1999
James R. Bertrand • 1974-1975	Nick C. Nichols • 1999-2000
Irvin (Bubba) Levy • 1975-1976	Danny Weingeist • 2000-2001
Don J. Tomasco • 1976-1977	John Schleider • 2001-2002
James M. Keegan • 1977-1978	Douglas A. Dawson • 2002-2003
W.B. "Bud" Rae • 1978-1979	Bill Marshall • 2003-2004
Richard Alfeld • 1979-1980	Fred Saunders • 2004-2005
Dallas Cantwell • 1980-1981	Meg Smith • 2005-2006
F. Ames Smith • 1981-1982	Ted Erck • 2006-2007
Richard E. Schuette, M.D. • 1982-1983	Bob Landauer • 2007-2008
Robert E. McFarland • 1983-1984	Tim Purcell • 2008-2009
Al Fairfield • 1984-1985	Steven Madden • 2009-2010
William L. Kottwitz • 1985-1986	Paul Peacock • 2010-2011
Dr. Thomas D. Creekmore • 1986-1987	Roni Atnipp • 2011-2012
Earle S. Alexander • 1987-1988	Leland Putterman • 2012-2013
Walter R. Evans • 1988-1989	Andrew Johnston • 2013-2014
Judge Michael T. McSpadden • 1989-1990	Brad Patt • 2014-2015
Albert S. Tabor Sr. • 1990-1991	Michael Monk • 2015-2016

HRC WOMEN'S ASSOCIATION PRESIDENTS

Betty Tuttle • 1968-1969	Joanne Naponic • 1992-1993
Sissy Sparks • 1969-1970	Cathy McGehee • 1993-1994
Delores Hornberger • 1970-1971	Carol Allen • 1994-1995
Ruth McGovern • 1971-1972	Carrie Woliver • 1995-1996
Sybil Stephens • 1972-1973	Lynn Guggoltz • 1996-1997
June Levy • 1973-1974	Charlotte Johns • 1997-1998
Nelle Patton • 1974-1975	Carol Vickery • 1998-1999
Maxine Mueller • 1975-1976	Stella Blackwell • 1999-2000
Linda Perlman • 1976-1977	Joy Wilcock • 2000-2001
Starlette Hollingsworth • 1977-1978	Cathy Lassetter • 2001-2002
Bette Moore • 1978-1979	Mary Ann Gralka • 2002-2003
Caroline Davis • 1979-1980	Meg Smith • 2003-2004
Jackie Stagg • 1980-1981	Kathy Zay • 2004-2005
Connie Schulgen • 1981-1982	Kathy Huddleston • 2005-2006
Anne Alexander • 1982-1983	Sue Bramlette • 2006-2007
Jan Nieland • 1983-1984	Donna Hinds • 2007-2008
Doris Bernard • 1984-1985	Meg Phipps • 2008-2009
Peggy McFarland • 1985-1986	Meg Phipps • 2009-2010
Joan McCleary • 1986-1987	Marcia Gsell • 2010-2011
Nancy Levicki • 1987-1988	Jamie Alford • 2011-2012
Holly Anderson • 1988-1989	Heidi Hedrick • 2012-2013
Bonnie Gray • 1989-1990	Staci Johnson • 2013-2014
Linda Nichols • 1990-1991	Gayette Eicher • 2014-2015
Patti Garrison • 1990-1991	Cathy Lassetter • 2015-2016

HRC MEN'S ASSOCIATION PRESIDENTS

Dan Crawford • 2013-2014

Tim Jordan • 2014-2015

► 1973,
HRC pool

HRC CURRENT AND FORMER TENNIS PROS

Doug Banks	Kicha Mazique
Moncief Benaji	Marlon Mazique
Chris Bovett	Mark Miller
Sue Bramlette	Tammy Morris
Jack Brasington	Richard Nesmith, Head Pro
Robby Clarkson	Guillermo Palmer
Thomas Cook, Head Pro	Jim Parker, Head Pro
Mitch Creekmore	Phillip Perez
Derik Crosser	Ross Persons
Owen Davidson, Head Pro	Robby Reneberg
Tony Dawson	Rocky Royer
Randy Druz	Otis Sadler
Jerry Evert	Carla Salazar
Jane Firbank Hernandez	Robin Sandage
Harry Fowler	Emily Schaefer
Sammy Giammalva Sr., Head Pro	Anat Schaehmon
Alex Graham	Mark Schultz
Craig Gold	Kai Siewrattan
Tom Gustafson	Jane Strnadle
Kevin Hedberg	Cliff Tyree
Lee Henson	Jerry Walters
Kristin Hess	Jim Ward
Ann Hopper	Betty Washington
John Hopper	Paris Watt
Manfried Jachmich	Troy Wethe
John Kirwan	Graham Whaling
Daryl Lerner	Craig Wilson

MEN'S SINGLES CLUB CHAMPIONS

Ronnie Fisher • 1977	John Burrmann • 1990	Ted Erck • 2004
Ed Austin • 1978	Rafael Rizo Patron • 1991	Ted Erck • 2005
Larry Briggs • 1979	Rafael Rizo Patron • 1992	Harry Fowler • 2006
Larry Briggs • 1980	Ted Erck • 1993	Danny Weingeist • 2007
Graham Whaling • 1981	Allan Boss • 1994	Danny Weingeist • 2008
Graham Wahling • 1982	Mickey Branisa • 1995	Leland Putterman • 2009
Richey Reneberg • 1983	Danny Weingeist • 1996	Leland Putterman • 2010
Richard Finger • 1984	Mickey Branisa • 1997	Robert Collins • 2011
Dale McCleary • 1985	Mickey Branisa • 1998	Darin Mast • 2012
Kirk Tomasco • 1986	Peter Svensson • 1999	Rafael Herrera • 2013
Mickey Branisa • 1987	Ted Erck • 2000	Danny Schnyder • 2014
Hans Paino • 1988	Peter Svensson • 2001	Chris Zolas • 2015
Jan Erik Paino • 1989	Ted Erck • 2002	
	Danny Weingeist • 2003	

MEN'S SINGLES A CHAMPIONS

Rick Reitz • 1977	Robert Blevins • 1990	Nick Stephens • 2005
Tim Goodwin • 1978	Bob McFarland • 1991	John Meredith • 2006
Tom Creekmore • 1979	Bill Pugh • 1992	Tim Jordan • 2007
Bob Stagg • 1980	Martin Lide • 1993	Luis Enrique Cuervo • 2008
A.L. Hernden • 1981	Keith Page • 1994	Eddie Perdomo • 2009
Bill Karol • 1982	Brian Gammill • 1995	Tim Jordan • 2010
Towson Ellis • 1983	John Schleider • 1996	Dave Stablein • 2011
A.L. Hernden • 1984	Todd Frnka • 1997	John Meredith • 2012
Bob McFarland • 1985	Marshall Rosenberg • 1998	Matt Dawson • 2013
Dave Wood • 1986	Arlo Van Denover • 1999	Javier Gonzalez • 2014
Bill Griffith • 1987	Brian Gammill • 2000	Matt Dawson • 2015
Read Boles • 1988	Dan Kalb • 2001	
Dave Wood • 1989	John Meredith • 2002	
	Keith Page • 2003	
	Doug Dawson • 2004	

MEN'S SINGLES B CHAMPIONS

Nick Nichols • 1977

Bob Alexander • 1978

John Hansen • 1979

Jim Elder • 1980

Don Mafrige • 1981

Hugh Wilfong • 1982

Gary Kob • 1983

Lynn Woods • 1984

Monty McDannald • 1985

Ben Roberts • 1986

Art Bell • 1987

Dirk Gralka • 1988

Sherman Hink • 1989

John Chambers • 1990

Doug Schaefer • 1991

Sherman Hink • 1992

Bob Murphy • 1993

Glenn Ballard • 1994

Sherman Hink • 1995

Albert Schneuwly • 1997

Lance Brown • 2002

Bob Gitomer • 2004

Steve Smith • 2005

Jim Pappas • 2006

Mike Calhoun • 2007

Anthony Tarantino • 2008

Brian Womac • 2009

Anthony Tarantino • 2010

Brian Womac • 2011

Paul Edmonds • 2012

Brian Krivan • 2013

Lucas Walker • 2014

Brian Womac • 2015

MEN'S SINGLES C CHAMPIONS

Doug Nicholson • 1977

Don Knowlton • 1978

Carrol Hunt • 1979

Mike Grant • 1980

Jeff Hubbard • 1985

Mark Hobson • 1986

Harvey Mohr • 1987

John Simmons • 1988

Terry Lesch • 1991

Warren Cross • 1992

Ray Hofker • 1993

Andy Medlenka • 1996

Dave Ressler • 2007

Greg Browne • 2010

Blane Bauch • 2011

MEN'S SINGLES SENIOR CHAMPIONS

Jesse Jefferies • 1977

Horst Manhard • 2000

Bob Landauer • 2001

Jesse Jefferies • 2004

Clark Reid • 2006

Clark Reid • 2008

Bob Landauer • 2009

John Williams • 2010

Ron Fisher • 2011

Ron Fisher • 2012

Ron Fisher • 2013

Andy Newton • 2015

MEN'S DOUBLES CLUB CHAMPIONS

1977	1986	1996	2006
John Been	Billy Fisher	Mitch Creekmore	Ted Erck
Richard Schuette	Ronnie Fisher	Danny Weingeist	Ryan McCleary
	1987		
1978	John Been	**1997**	**2007**
Fred Gradin	Ronnie Fisher	Mitch Creekmore	Ryan McCleary
Leland Putterman		Danny Weingeist	Leland Putterman
	1988		
1979	John Been	**1998**	**2008**
John Been	Blair Neller	Richard Robert	Ryan McCleary
Richard Schuette		Peter Svensson	Leland Putterman
	1989		
1980	Jay Evert	**1999**	**2009**
Roger Gruggett	Billy Fisher	Mitch Creekmore	Ted Erck
Dale McCleary		Paul Nunley	Andy Johnston
	1990		
1981	Mitch Creekmore	**2000**	**2010**
Larry Briggs	Kermit Smith	Allan Boss	Graydon Oliver
Graham Whaling		Danny Weingeist	Danny Weingeist
	1991		
1982	Jay Evert	**2001**	**2011**
Roger Gruggett	Leland Putterman	Leland Putterman	William Barker
Graham Whaling		Danny Weingeist	David Toney
	1992		
1983	John Been	**2002**	**2012**
Dale McCleary	Ryan McCleary	Dan Courson	Ted Erck
Graham Whaling		Mitch Creekmore	Andy Johnston
	1993		
1984	Leland Putterman	**2003**	**2013**
Dale McCleary	Danny Weingeist	Dennis Cahill	William Barker
Graham Whaling		Danny Weingeist	Chris Zolas
	1994		
1985	Allan Boss	**2004**	**2014**
Billy Fisher	Ed Ruffin	Ted Erck	Daniel Riner
Ronnie Fisher		Ryan McCleary	Alex White
	1995		
	Leland Putterman	**2005**	
	Danny Weingeist	Ted Erck	
		Ryan McCleary	

MEN'S DOUBLES A CHAMPIONS

1977 Ron Latta Alex Pegues	**1986** Tom Creekmore Towson Ellis	**1996** Bob Bramlette Keith Page	**2007** Eddie Perdomo Scott Stafford
1978 Cecil Christensen Towson Ellis	**1987** Bob Garrison Bob Huff	**1997** Dick Eicher Mark Holmes	**2008** Doug Dawson John Meredith
1979 Bob Alexander Dale Culwell	**1988** Louis Brandt Bill Marshall	**1999** Keith Page Mike Stavinoha	**2009** Ron Latta Nick Stephens
1980 Tom Cook Richard Meyers	**1989** Robert Blevins John Goodpasture	**2000** Todd Frnka John Schleider	**2010** Ron Latta Keith Page
1981 Ron Latta Richard Meyers	**1990** Roger Anderson Dick Corbin	**2001** Joe Baden Read Boles	**2011** Paul Schiebl Dave Stablein
1982 Clyde Buck Bob Stagg	**1991** Tom Cox Mike Pfeifle	**2002** Doug Dawson John Meredith	**2012** Ty Hoffer Dave Stablein
1983 Richard Meyers Ed Ruffin	**1992** Bob Cline John Goodpasture	**2003** Brad Dawson Doug Dawson	**2013** William Brice Ty Hoffer
1984 Ron Latta Sid Nachlas	**1993** Hager Bryant Keith Page	**2004** Tim Purcell Nick Stephens	**2014** Thomas Orser Scott Stafford
1985 Richard Meyers Ed Ruffin	**1994** Towson Ellis Clark Reid	**2005** Doug Dawson John Meredith	
	1995 Dick Eicher Mark Holmes	**2006** Doug Dawson Brian Gammill	

◄
1972,
Cleo James
with HRC
players in
the snow

MEN'S DOUBLES B CHAMPIONS

1977	1986	1996	2006
Mike Hill	Ron Mafrige	Friedrich Brenckmann	Jim Gosnell
Leo Kissner	Hugh Wilfong	Albert Schneuwly	Jay Morrison

1978	1987	1997	2007
Bob Alexander	John Chambers	Josh Green	Joel Phipps
Jim Metz	Lynn Woods	Horst Manhard	Brian Womac

1979	1988	1998	2008
Tom Mitchell	Chuck Beckham	Fred Snyder	Sherman Hink
Ed Tribble	Noel Fruge	Craig Wasserman	Lynn Woods

1980	1989	1999	2009
Gary Levering	Max Goldberg	John Harrell	Bob Gitomer
Doug Nicholson	Jim Metz	Byrd Larberg	Danny Stephens

1981	1990	2000	2010
Charles Berry	Sherman Hink	Friedrich Brenckmann	Bob Gitomer
Hugh Wilfong	Bill Howell	Craig Wasserman	Brian Savino

1982	1991	2001	2011
Skip McBride	John Green	Mike Calhoun	Alan Ratterree
Richard Royds	Horst Manhard	Mark Lamp	David Fisher

1983	1992	2002	2012
Bob Jenkins	Bob Murphy	Drew Cantwell	Greg Browne
Bernie Riviere	Ed Murphy	Bob Koush	Danny Stephens

1984	1993	2003	2013
Fred McCown	John Chambers	Jim Gosnell	Malcom Paterson
Dave Wood	Bill Kottwitz	Jay Morrison	Greg Browne

1985	1994	2004	2014
Larry Ainsworth	John Green	Lance Brown	Greg Browne
Don Mafrige	Horst Manhard	Waters Davis	Bob Gitomer

1995	2005
John Harrell	Lance Brown
Jim Levicki	Dave Ressler

MEN'S DOUBLES C CHAMPIONS

1977	1979	1985
Gus Comiskey	Carrol Hunt	Charles Goolsbee
Charlie Melton	Ken Minter	Charles Peterman

1978		2010
Charles Goolsbee	1980	Craig Beasley
Charles Peterman	Joe Mattei	Brian Smith
	John Stieneker	

1981
John Chambers
Jeff Hubbard

MEN'S DOUBLES SENIOR CHAMPIONS

1996	2010	2013
Chuck Beckham	Tom Whitehead	Ron Fisher
Towson Ellis	John Williams	Bob Landauer

2008	2011	2014
Bob Landauer	Ron Latta	Bill Fisher
Clark Reid	Bob Stagg	Ron Fisher

2012
Ron Latta
Bob Stagg

WOMEN'S SINGLES CLUB CHAMPIONS

Sue Shaper • 1977	Margaret Kitchen • 1997	Annabel Fowler • 2008
Cathie Childers • 1980	Christie Schweer • 1998	Mindy Voyles • 2009
Cathie McGee • 1983	Daryl Lerner • 1999	Ria Gerger • 2010
Marcy Taub • 1984	Daryl Lerne • 2000	Ria Gerger • 2011
Marcy Taub • 1985	Margaret Kitchen • 2001	Ria Gerger • 2012
Emily Schaefer • 1990	Erin Murphy • 2002	Mindy Voyles • 2013
Emily Schaefer • 1991	Lenora Wright • 2003	Tammy Morris • 2014
Daryl Lerner • 1992	Georgiana Smyser • 2004	Correne Loeffler • 2015
Christie Bramlette Pettit • 1993	Annabel Fowler • 2005	
Daryl Lerner • 1994	Annabel Fowler • 2006	
Daryl Lerner • 1995	Annabel Fowler • 2007	

WOMEN'S SINGLES A CHAMPIONS

Gundi McCandless • 1977	Colleen Hagen • 1993	Julie Gillaspie • 2006
Bette Moore • 1978	J.J. Bubb • 1994	Kristin Waring • 2007
Nancy Mafrige • 1979	Colleen Hagen • 1995	Kathy Ratterree • 2008
Joan Egan • 1980	Susan Strohmeyer • 1996	Jennifer Kruse • 2009
Holly Anderson • 1981	Colleen Hagen • 1997	Jackie Busa • 2011
Daisy Quayle • 1982	Susan Strohmeyer • 1998	Debra Baker • 2012
Rosemary Estenson • 1983	Susan Strohmeyer • 2000	Courtney Walker • 2013
Sandra Evans • 1984	Luean Anthony • 2001	Debra Baker • 2014
Daisy Quayle • 1990	Julie Gillaspie • 2002	Jackie Busa • 2015
Pat Walzel • 1991	Colleen Hagen • 2003	
Lovie Beard • 1992	Julie Page • 2004	
	Kaari Wicklund • 2005	

WOMEN'S SINGLES B CHAMPIONS

Connie Colley • 1977

Nancy Levicki • 1978

Mary Platt • 1979

Julie Williams • 1980

Ann Dykes • 1982

Deanna Lambert • 1984

Sherry Gruggett • 1990

Michele Brenckman • 1991

Peggy Hunt • 1992

Susan Boss • 1993

Cathy Lassetter • 1994

Mary Ann Gralka • 1995

Beverly Pletcher • 1997

Andrea Bauer • 2000

Sally Goldberg • 2002

Donna Hinds • 2005

Stephanie Dickinson • 2007

Jennifer Kruse • 2008

Jackie Busa • 2009

Katherine Richards • 2010

Denise Dunham • 2011

Gaby Tormo • 2012

Kathryn Smyser • 2013

Fay Lewis • 2015

WOMEN'S SINGLES C CHAMPIONS

Pili Oliver • 1977

Donna Legro • 1978

Sue Sheeler • 1979

Betty Rose • 1980

Deanna Lambert • 1983

Gwen Bruner • 1984

Kathy Scanlan • 1991

Kappa Muldoon • 1992

Cathy Lassetter • 1993

Margaret Lyus • 1997

Julie Gillaspie • 1999

Merrill Eliff • 2008

Debbie Bragg • 2010

Hemmat Maguire • 2014

WOMEN'S SINGLES SENIOR CHAMPIONS

Bambi Schuette • 2008

Bambi Schuette • 2010

Alisa Slack • 2012

Betsy Beasley • 2014

◀

2013, Tommy Ho serving at the WOTT

2014, Earl Beard at the Lovie Beard Celebration of Life at HRC

2015, HRC founding and charter members at 50th anniversary get-together

(top row) Valerie Ziegenfuss, Billie Jean King, Nancy Richey, Peaches Bartkowicz (bottom row) Judy Dalton, Kerry Melville, Rosie Casals, Gladys Heldman, Kristy Pigeon

HOUSTON RACQUET CLUB
BIRTHPLACE OF THE
WOMEN'S PROFESSIONAL TENNIS TOUR

In 1970, eight of the leading women players of the era accepted the token sum of one dollar, thereby becoming contract pros and committing themselves irrevocably to the fledgling professional game. Under the direction of Gladys Heldman and in direct defiance of the USTA, HRC hosted the first tournament of what would eventually become the highly successful Virginia Slims Tour. This tournament was also noteworthy because it was the first time the USTA had ever denied a sanction to a tournament. As a result of their efforts, these courageous women laid the groundwork for the modern professional tour with its rich purses and worldwide media coverage. We are honored to celebrate this auspicious event.

Presented by
The Women's Association of the Houston Racquet Club

WOMEN'S DOUBLES CLUB CHAMPIONS

1977	1986	1997	2005
Leslie Creekmore	Emily Schuette	J.J. Bubb	Annabel Fowler
Diana Zody	Marcy Taub	Charlotte Johns	Heidi Gerger
1978	**1987**	**1998**	**2006**
Leslie Creekmore	Emily Schaefer	Colleen Hagen	Sue Bramlette
Diana Zody	Marcy Taub	Charlotte Johns	Annabel Fowler
1979	**1988**	**1999**	**2007**
Bambi Schuette	Susan Griffith	Sue Bramlette	Heidi Gerger
Sue Shaper	Judy Job	Lenora Wright	Ria Gerger
1980	**1990**	**2000**	**2008**
Leslie Creekmore	Emily Schaefer	Julie Page	Sue Bramlette
Diana Zody	Bambi Schuette	Susan Strohmeyer	Heidi Gerger
1981	**1991**	**2001**	**2009**
Cathie Childers	Emily Schaefer	Judy Job	Mindy Voyles
Bambi Schuette	Bambi Schuette	Lenora Wright	Lenora Wright
1982	**1993**	**2002**	**2011**
Cathie McGee	Jennifer Embree	Judy Job	Julie Page
Bambi Schuette	Judy Embree	Lenora Wright	Mindy Rice
1984	**1994**	**2003**	**2012**
Leslie Creekmore	Sue Bramlette	Sue Bramlette	Julie Page
Judy Job	Christie Bramlette Pettit	Margaret Kitchen	Mindy Rice
1985	**1996**	**2004**	**2014**
Sue Bramlette	Judy Job	Annabel Fowler	Tammy Morris
Bambi Schuette	Daisy Quayle	Heidi Gerger	Jennifer Toney

Plaque that hangs in the Grill Lobby honoring the start of the Women's Professional Tennis Tour at HRC

1972,
Caroline
Baumann

12. CAROLINE B.

WOMEN'S DOUBLES A CHAMPIONS

1977 Tally McNay Judy Phillips	**1985** J.J. Bubb Joan Eldridge	**1996** Susan Branisa Julie Thayer	**2005** Dayna Erck Laura Gauss
1978 Eileen Eastham Rita Madden	**1986** Patti Garrison Ann Gibbs	**1997** Joan Eldridge Mary Ann Gralka	**2006** Tonja Brown Kathy Ratterree
1979 Ann Chittick Julie Whitaker	**1988** June Levy Laura Ragsdale	**1998** Dayna Erck Ellen Parker	**2007** Roni Atnipp Jennifer Hill
1980 Camille Lartigue Jeff Miller	**1989** Nancy Levicki Daisy Quayle	**1999** Buff Hauck Kathy O'Brien	**2008** Stephanie Dickinson Vickey Rocher
1981 Nancy Dickey Margaret Laroe	**1990** Holly Anderson Ann Gibbs	**2000** Dayna Erck Susanna Schultz	**2009** Betsy Beasley Ginger Dailey
1982 Rita Madden Gundi McCandless	**1991** Patti Garrison Susie Townsend	**2001** Andrea Bauer Macey Krpec	**2010** Maude Dawson Patty Harris
1983 Sue Bramlette Nancy Levicki	**1993** J.J. Bubb Joanna Millinor	**2002** Dayna Erck Laura Gauss	**2011** Lisa Kroll Jennifer Kruse
1984 Joan Bryant Donna Griffiths	**1994** Susan Branisa Julie Thayer	**2003** Maude Dawson Cindy Reeter	**2013** Lisa Kroll Jennifer Kruse
	1995 Colleen Hagen Juanita Smith	**2004** Maude Dawson Laura Gauss	

WOMEN'S DOUBLES B CHAMPIONS

1977 Connie Colley Ceacy Hailey	**1987** Deanna Lambert Jackie Wood	**2002** Wendy Hunsaker Juli Ruben
1978 Jackie Dienna Maxine Fox	**1988** Ann Jones Dorothy Mitchell	**2005** Lee Ann Holmes Kathy Ratterree
1979 Connie Colley Ruth Vine	**1990** Dawn Burns Lucy Kuhn	**2006** Jackie Busa Stephanie Dickinson
1980 Kay Boone Harriet Friend	**1991** Michele Brenckmann Colleen Hagen	**2007** Leslie Iler Jennifer Kruse
1982 Sue Sheeler Julie Williams	**1993** Danuta Chacko Cynthia O'Malley	**2008** Stephanie Dickinson Vickey Rocher
1983 Cathy Brewton Judy McDannald	**1994** Cathy Lassetter Bootsie Le Feuvre	**2009** Vicki Locascio Gaby Tormo
1984 TJ Beck Charlotte Marshall	**1995** Lea Bell Nadia Branisa	**2011** Vicki Locascio Gaby Tormo
1985 Joanne Cone Joanna Millinor	**1996** Sheryl Fisher Carol Vickery	**2013** Kathy Pappas Jo Soanes
	2000 Macey Krpec Tori Schroer	

WOMEN'S DOUBLES C CHAMPIONS

1977
Martha Fahnoe
Wanda Fielder

1978
Joan Eldridge
Donna Legro

1979
Penny Jones
Jeanelle Waldrop

1982
B.D. McAndrew
Susan Smith

1983
Ann Jones
Dorothy Mitchell

1984
Bonnie Gray
Judy Pereira

1985
Deanna Lambert
Phyllis Richard

1988
Julie Gibson
Troice Jenckes

1996
Becky Boylan
Ann Marie Wood

1998
Andrea Bauer
Pam Lamp

2008
Vicki Locascio
Gaby Tormo

2012
Tiziana Velasco
Anna Weiner

WOMEN'S SENIOR CLUB CHAMPIONS

2011
Lovie Beard
Alisa Slack

2013
Betsy Beasley
Bambi Schuette

SPECIAL THANKS

To the following HRC friends, without whose generous contributions of time, energy, expertise, and guidance, *Remembering Our Past & Celebrating Our Future: Houston Racquet Club 50th Anniversary* could not have been realized:

Thomas Preuml, Cathy Lassetter, and Jean Northey – Thank you for your time and effort in tracking down the details and pictures for this book as well as your dedication to the Club and its members.

Paul Peacock and Meg Smith – Your talents in helping build the concept and editing assistance were invaluable in creating such a unique history book.

Ron Fisher – The amazing *Tennis Titans* chapter of this book is your creation. Thank you for the hours and hours you spent reading through years of tennis journals building the impressive list of HRC tennis superstars.

Bob Shealor – Thank you for helping in so many ways to bring the story of HRC to life through your interviews of members and staff.

To all the members of the 50th Anniversary Committee – Mitch Creekmore, Tom Eaton, Ron Latta, Ryan McCleary, Leland Putterman, Bambi Schuette, Adelaide Smith, Bob Stagg, Mindy Voyles, and Kathy Zay – A heartfelt thank you for your work in making the Club's celebration year fun and exciting.

To all of you, I am thankful for your friendship and support during the past two years of development and planning for the 50th anniversary celebration – especially for the help in putting this book together.

Roni

Roni Atnipp
Chair, HRC 50th Anniversary Committee

INDEX

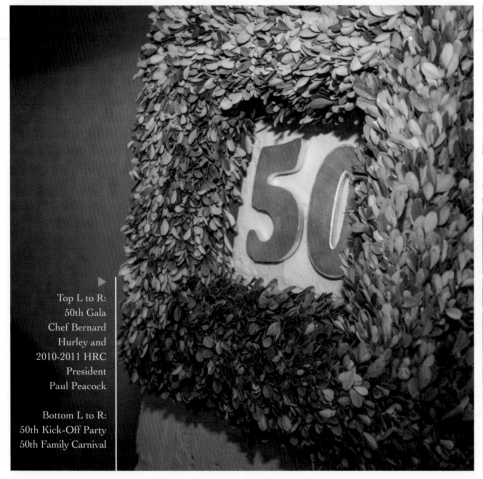

Top L to R:
50th Gala
Chef Bernard
Hurley and
2010-2011 HRC
President
Paul Peacock

Bottom L to R:
50th Kick-Off Party
50th Family Carnival

▼

Top L to R: Luncheon honoring
three players of the "Original 9"
50th Gala

Bottom L to R: Members
of all ages enjoying the 50th
Anniversary Exhibition Match